T HE QUEST FOR FIRE, considered by many the finest of J. H. Rosny's portrayals of prehistoric life, is the story of three young warriors of the Oulhamr tribe who journey through vast, unknown expanses to recover life-giving Fire, which has been extinguished by an enemy tribe. It is a powerful and compelling story of prehistoric struggle and man's first agonizing steps toward civilization.

◄◄ The Quest for Fire ►►

The Quest for Fire

A Novel of Prehistoric Times

J. H. Rosny | *Pictures by J. O. Bercher*

TRANSLATION BY HAROLD TALBOTT

Pantheon Books

*To Theodore Duret
this journey into
far-distant prehistory.*

HIS ADMIRER AND FRIEND,

J. H. Rosny

CONTENTS

◄◄ Part One ►►

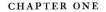

The Fire Dies

THROUGH the terrible night the band of Oulhamrs fled. What had befallen them, wounded and exhausted, made all effort seem useless: the Fire was dead. They had tended the Fire in three cages; four women and two warriors had fed it with fuel night and day. Even in the darkest days the Fire was given the material to live by. Sheltered from rain and flood, it had crossed rivers and swamps, never failing to burn, a blue flame at dawn and blood red at night. The sight of it had power to chase away the black lion and the yellow, the cave bear and the gray bear, the mammoth, tiger, and leopard; the red fangs of fire protected man against the whole vast world. Fire was the source of all delights. It drew a delicious odor from meat; by it the points of spears were made hard, and hard stone could be split. Fire warmed the body and made it rested and strong; it gave reassurance to the band through rustling forests, across endless savannas, in the dark depths of caves. Fire was father, guardian, and savior. But it was more ferocious and terrifying than the mammoths themselves when it escaped from its cage and devoured the trees.

It was dead!

The enemy had destroyed two cages; in the third cage, while they fled, the band had seen the Fire fade and become small, too weak to eat up the swamp grass, flickering like an animal that is sick. Finally it became a tiny reddish insect bruised by every gust of wind. It went out, and the Oulhamrs, dispossessed, fled through the autumn night. There were no stars. The heavy sky and the water touched oppressively; the creepers stretched out their clammy tendrils; reptiles were heard scuttling about. A few of them — men, women, and children — sank in the mire and disappeared. As far as possible the band stuck to a higher and firmer line of country, seeking out fording points and dry spots. The way had been familiar to three generations of the Oulhamrs, but they needed the light of the stars. Toward dawn they approached the savanna.

A chill light filtered through the chalky clouds. The wind was swirling over water as thick as pitch, full of algae swollen like pustules. Here sluggish saurians wallowed among the flowering rushes and water lilies. A heron flew up into an ash tree, and there before them appeared the savanna with its trembling growth, stretching into the distance beneath a russet mist.

The men drew themselves up, less exhausted, and having crossed through the rushes, they found themselves in the grass, on firm ground.

Once the deadly tension was lifted, many of them turned into inert animals. They tumbled to the ground and sank into sleep. The women resisted better than the men; those who had lost their children in the swamp howled like wolves; all of them had a sinister sense of the downfall of the race and the harsh days to come. Some of the women had managed to save their babies, and these raised them in their arms toward the clouds.

In the new light Faouhm counted his band with the aid of fingers and sticks. Each stick stood for the fingers of both hands. He counted badly, but he perceived that there remained only two sticks of warriors, over two sticks of women, less than two sticks of children, and a few old men.

Despite his own strength, Faouhm was in despair. He no longer had faith in his height or his great arms. His broad face covered with tough hairs, his yellow eyes like a leopard's, betrayed defeat. He examined his wounds from enemy spears; now and then he licked the blood which still flowed from his forearm.

As with every man in his defeat, his mind reverted to the moment when he might have conquered. The Oulhamrs had hurled themselves forward for the slaughter, and Faouhm himself had bashed heads with his club. They were about to wipe out the men and carry off the women, killing the enemy's fire, and then they would hunt on new savannas and in abundant forests. What had become of their advantage? Why had the Oulhamrs spun around in terror, why was it their bones that got broken, their guts that were torn out, their lungs and throats that screamed in agony, as the enemy invaded their camp and overturned the sacred Fires. Thus the questions slowly emerged in Faouhm's dull mind. He set upon the memory like a hyena upon a carcass. He could not abide defeat, not sensing himself any less energetic, courageous, or ferocious.

The light attained its full strength, rolling across the swamp, illuminating the muddy tracks and drying out the grasslands. The joy of morning was in the savanna. The water looked lighter, less evil and dangerous; it sent out long ripples of malachite and pearl, displaying pale sulphurs and glints of mica. Algae were in triumphant abundance; the water sparkled with white and yellow water lilies; iris stood tall, and marshy euphorbia, yellow loosestrife, and flowering rushes grew profusely. There were broad gulfs of ranunculus with beds of tufty or-pine winding through them, and sedge, pink willow herb, cresses, and sundew. Here were jungles of reeds and willows where waterfowl swarmed, sandpipers, teals, plovers, lapwings shimmering like jade. Herons stalked the banks of the rust-colored creeks; chattering cranes frisked about on a headland; barbed carp attacked tenches; and the last dragonflies spun about in lazuli zig-zags, making strokes of green flame.

Faouhm considered his people. Covered with yellow clay and green algae, scarlet with blood, the band gave off an odor of fever and rotting flesh. Some of the men were twisted like pythons, others stretched out like saurians. Their wounds were turning black, hideous body wounds and worse ones on the head, where they were enlarged by the blood-reddened sponge of hair. Nearly all of them would recover, those who had been hit worst having succumbed on the other shore or perished in the water.

Taking his eyes off the sleeping warriors, Faouhm examined those who were feeling defeat more bitterly than exhaustion. Many showed the fine stature of the Oulhamrs. They had heavy faces, low craniums, fierce jaws. Their skin was tawny rather than black; almost all had hairy chests and limbs. The subtlety of their senses included smell, in which they matched animals. They had big eyes, often ferocious and sometimes haggard, but beautiful in the children and some young girls.

Faouhm raised his arms to the sun with a long yell.

"What will become of the Oulhamrs without Fire?" he cried. "How shall they live on the savanna and in the forest? Who will defend them against shadows and winter blasts? They will have to eat raw meat and bitter plants, never to warm their limbs, and their spearheads will remain soft. The lion, the saber-toothed tiger, the bear, the tiger, the giant hyena will eat them alive during the night. Who will recapture Fire? That man shall be

Faouhm's brother; he shall have three shares of the game, four shares of the booty; he will receive Gammla as his portion, daughter of my sister, and if I die, he will command."

Then Naoh, son of the Leopard, rose and said:

"Let me have two warriors swift of foot and I will go and seize Fire from the sons of the Mammoth, or from the man-eaters who hunt by the banks of the Great River."

Faouhm did not look upon him with favor. Naoh was the greatest in stature of the Oulhamrs. His shoulders were broadening still. There was no more agile warrior; none could outrun him. He had struck down Mouh, son of the Urus, whose strength approached Faouhm's. And Faouhm feared him.

Naoh disliked the chief, but he thrilled at the sight of Gammla, stretched out, lithe and mysterious, with her hair like foliage. If he had her for his woman, he would not mistreat her, for he did not like to see fear spreading over a face and making people strangers.

At another time Faouhm would have found Naoh's words unwelcome. But the catastrophe had brought him down. Perhaps alliance with the son of the Leopard would be a good thing; if not, he would not hesitate to put him to death. So, turning toward the young man, he said, "Faouhm has but one message. If you bring back Fire you shall have Gammla without giving any ransom in exchange. You shall be Faouhm's son." He held up his hand as he spoke slowly and roughly with scorn. Then he signaled to Gammla. She came forward, trem-

(8)

bling, raising her fiery, expressive eyes. She was aware that Naoh stalked her in the grass and amid the shadows. When he appeared at a bend in the grassland as if he was going to fling himself upon her, she was afraid of him. Sometimes, however, the sight of him wasn't disagreeable. She hoped at once that he would die under the blows of the man-eaters and that he would bring back Fire.

The rough hand of Faouhm came down on the girl's shoulder. "Who is better made among the daughters of men?" he cried in his savage pride. "She can shoulder a doe, walk without weakening from dawn to dusk, withstand hunger and thirst, dress animal hides, and swim across a lake; she will bear unconquerable children. If Naoh brings Fire back, he will come and take her without giving axes, horns, shells, or furs."

Then Aghoo, son of the Aurochs, hairiest of the Oulhamr tribe, came forward: "Aghoo wants to conquer Fire. He shall go with his brothers in search of the enemies across the river. He shall die by the axe, spear, jaws of the tiger, or claws of the giant lion, or he will return Fire to the Oulhamrs, without which they are weak like stags or antelopes."

Nothing of his face was visible but a mouth bordered by raw flesh and a pair of murderous eyes. His squat stature exaggerated the length of his arms and the enormous width of his shoulders. His whole being expressed a brutal strength, tireless and without pity. No one knew the limit of his strength: he had not used it against either Faouhm or Mouh or Naoh. It was known to be enormous. He never tried it in any peaceful contest: all who had crossed his path had fallen, whether he had stopped at mutilating one of their limbs or had done away with them and added their skulls to his trophies. He lived apart from the band with two brothers, hairy like himself, and several women reduced to servitude. Although the Oulhamrs naturally practiced harshness toward themselves and ferocity toward others, they feared the excessive degree to which the sons of the Aurochs carried these virtues.

Faouhm hated Aghoo as much as the son of the Leopard did, and he had more fear of him. The shaggy and cunning strength of the brothers seemed unconquerable. If one of the three wanted a man to die, all of them wanted it; whoever declared war on them must perish or else wipe them all out.

Faouhm answered with rough deference: "If the Aurochs' son brings Fire back to the Oulhamrs, he shall take Gammla with no ransom; he shall be the second man in the band, whom all warriors shall obey in the chief's absence."

Aghoo listened grimly; turning his shaggy face toward Gammla, he studied her. His round eyes grew hard and menacing.

"The daughter of the Swamp will belong to the Aurochs' son; anyone who lays a hand on her shall be destroyed."

These words angered Naoh. Violently accepting the challenge, he shouted, "She will belong to the one who brings back Fire!"

"Aghoo will bring it back!"

They stared at each other. Till that day there had been no cause for quarrel between them. Their consciousness of each other's strength had kept them apart, and without common interests or an immediate source of rivalry they never encountered each other nor hunted together. Now Faouhm's speech had caused hatred. Naoh grasped his axe in the left hand and his spear in the right. When Aghoo hurled the challenge, his brothers silently came forward, looking sneaky and dangerous. They strangely resembled him but were even wilder, with patches of reddish hair and eyes that were cloudy like the covers of beetle wings. Their suppleness was as alarming as their strength.

All three were stalking Naoh, ready to kill. But a cry rose from the warriors. Even those who blamed Naoh for the mildness of his hatreds did not wish to see him die after the destruction of so many Oulhamrs, and since he promised to bring back Fire. He was known to abound with stratagems, to be tireless, and able to keep alive the feeblest flame, making it shoot up from the ashes: many had faith in his chances. In truth, Aghoo too possessed the patience and guile to bring undertakings to conclusion, and the Oulhamrs understood the usefulness of a double attempt. They rose up in a mob, and Goun the Dry-Bones gave expression to the hazy notions of the crowd:

"Do the Oulhamrs want to disappear from the earth? Do they forget that enemies and floods have destroyed so many warriors? All those who can carry the axe, spear, and club must live. Naoh and Aghoo are strong among those who hunt in the savanna: if one of them dies, the Oulhamrs will be weakened more than if numbers of others perished . . . The daughter of the Swamp will serve the one who brings Fire back to us."

"So be it!" rough voices seconded.

And the women shouted, "Gammla shall belong to the one who captures Fire!"

Aghoo shrugged. He despised the crowd but judged it untimely to stand up to it. Sure of outstripping Naoh, he would wait for a better opportunity to combat his rival and do away with him. His chest swelled with confidence.

As the sun rose higher, Aghoo and Naoh made ready to depart. The Hairy Ones carried club, axe, spear, and the flint-tipped javelin. Naoh, who counted on guile rather than force, had passed up sturdy warriors for two agile youths, Gaw and Nam, who could run long distances. Each one had an axe, a spear, and javelins. For himself Naoh added an oak club, a whole branch which had merely been roughed down and hardened in the fire. This was the weapon he preferred over all the others, and which he pitted against even the huge flesh-eaters.

First Faouhm addressed the Aurochs: "Aghoo saw the light before the Leopard's son. He will choose the route. If he heads toward the Twin Rivers, Naoh will circle the marsh at sunset . . . and if he circles the marsh, Naoh will head for the Twin Rivers."

"Aghoo does not know his route yet!" protested the Hairy One. "He is searching for Fire; he can go in the morning toward the swamp. How does the hunter who pursues the boar know where he shall kill it?"

"Let Aghoo change routes later," interposed Goun, whom the crowd gave a muttered backing. "He cannot leave in the direction of the sunset and the Twin Rivers at the same time. He must choose!"

In his obscure consciousness the son of the Aurochs realized that it would be a mistake, not to stand up to the chief, but to awaken Naoh's mistrust. Turning his wolflike face to the crowd he cried, "Aghoo will set out toward the setting sun." And making a blunt gesture to his brothers, he set out along the edge of the swamp.

Naoh did not make up his mind so quickly. He wanted to feel the image of Gammla in his eyes still. She was standing under an ash tree behind the group of elders. Naoh stepped forward; he saw her face turned toward the savanna. She had twisted marsh flowers in her hair, and a water lily the color of the moon; a glow seemed to emanate from her skin, more vivid than that of cool rivers and the green wood of trees.

Naoh's heart swelled so that he was choked with tenderness and anger; all those who separated him from Gammla seemed as odious as the sons of the Mammoth or the man-eaters. He raised his axe and said, "Daughter of the Swamp, Naoh shall not return, he will disappear in the earth, the sea, the bellies of hyenas, or he will bring back Fire to the Oulhamrs. He will bring shells to Gammla, blue stones, leopards' teeth, and aurochs' horns." At these words she gave the warrior a look full of a child's delight. But Faouhm, growing impatient, said, "The sons of the Aurochs have disappeared behind the poplars."

So Naoh and his companions set out toward the south.

CHAPTER TWO

The Mammoth and the Aurochs

NAOH, Gaw, and Nam walked all day over the savanna. It was at its period of growth. Grasses followed upon grasses as waves succeed each other on the sea. They bent beneath breaths of wind, crackled in the sunlight, and gave off innumerable scents. Here a hill would rise, followed by a hollow; then a stagnant pool; a solitary rock would loom in the shape of a mastodon. Antelopes, hares, and saigas dashed by; bustards and partridges flew up, wood pigeons glided, and cranes and crows; horses, wild asses, and elk galloped in herds.

A gray bear with the movements of a great ape and a rhinoceros, stronger than a tiger and almost as terrible as a giant lion, prowled about the green earth; aurochs appeared on the horizon.

In the evening Naoh, Nam, and Gaw camped at the foot of a mound; they could see nothing but the waves of grass unfurling. The earth was flat and melancholy, while in the vast skies the sunset composed and dispersed every formation of light and clouds. A purple gulf remained for a long time deep in the sky, where the stars like little sparkling stones appeared one after another, and the evening breeze started up.

Accustomed to bonfires at night which were like barriers of light set against the sea of shadows, Naoh became aware of his puniness. The gray bear might turn up, or the leopard, tiger, or lion, even though they rarely came into the open spaces of the savanna. A herd of aurochs would be like a flood drowning their fragile human flesh; numbers gave the wolves the strength of the giant beasts and hunger armed them with courage.

The warriors fed on raw flesh. It was a gloomy meal, for they loved the smell of roast meat. Afterward Naoh took the first watch. He breathed the night with his whole being. His nostrils perceived the breath of flowers, the pleasant scent of grass, the stench of wild beasts, the stale or musky odor of reptiles. His skin responded to a thousand changes from cold to hot, from dampness to dryness.

In the dark he watched for the deadly fangs and claws and the gleaming eyes of the flesh-eaters. Many recognized men as powerful animals and did not waste time on them. Hyenas passed by with jaws worse than those of lions, but they did not like a fight and were looking for dead flesh. A pack of wolves circled and for a long time howled around the mound. They made a few menacing passes, one of them sometimes sneaking up close, but they were afraid at first to attack these erect beasts. Then slowly the ring tightened; their yelps became less frequent and their breathing more rapid. Naoh took a handful of earth and hurled it at the nearest animal, yelling, "We have spears and clubs that can destroy bears, aurochs, and lions!"

The wolf was hit on the muzzle and, surprised by the sounds, ran away. The others called to each other and appeared to take council. Naoh threw another handful of earth. "You are too weak to fight the Oulhamrs! The next wolf who comes near will spill his guts."

Aroused by their leader's voice, Nam and Gaw stood up. These new silhouettes made the wolves retreat.

Naoh walked on for several days, avoiding attacks. These grew more frequent as they came closer to the forest. Although it was still a few days' journey away, its nearness was indicated by patches of trees and by the appearance of the giant beasts. The Oulhamrs noted the tiger and the giant panther. The nights became agonizing. The men set to work long before sunset surrounding themselves with obstacles; they searched for hollows, boulders, and thickets, and they avoided trees. On the fourth and fifth days they suffered from thirst. The earth offered no stream or pool. The desert grass grew pale, and dry reptiles glittered among the stones. Insects swooped down on the warriors' skins and stung them.

When the shadows of the fifth day lengthened, the earth became fresh and soft, the scent of water came down from the hills, and a herd of aurochs was seen traveling south. Then Naoh said to his companions, "We will drink before sundown. The aurochs are heading for a watering place."

Nam, son of the Poplar, and Gaw, son of the Saiga, needed to be given courage and confidence; in exchange they offered their docility. They were quick to forget suffering and enjoy pleasure. A leader could derive dependable services from them; it sufficed for them to know his will and his courage. Since their departure they had grown attached to Naoh. He sensed this and from their attachment he drew further strength.

Long shadows spread from the forest trees, the grass abounded with sap, and the setting sun lit up the herd of aurochs like a flood of tawny waters.

Naoh's last doubts disappeared: there beyond the notch in the hills was the watering place. Nam and Gaw knew it too, their nostrils flaring with the whiffs of freshness.

"We have to beat the aurochs," said Naoh.

For he was afraid that the watering place would be narrow and that the huge animals would take up the whole edge. The three men sped up to get to the hollow in the hills before the herd.

The animals advanced slowly because of their great

numbers, the caution of the old bulls, and the tiredness of the young. The Oulhamrs gained distance. Other creatures were using the same tactic; they saw light-footed saigas dart by, wild sheep, wild asses, and diagonally to them, a herd of horses. A number of them had already crossed the pass.

Naoh got a wide advance on the aurochs, so they could drink without hurrying. Nam and Gaw kept speeding up as their thirst grew stronger. They skirted the hill and entered the pass. The water came into view, the life-giving mother, more beneficent even than fire and less cruel. It was almost a lake, extending to the foot of a chain of rocks, with peninsulas cutting in, fed from the right by a river, and falling into a chasm on the left. There was access to it from three directions: from the river, the pass the Oulhamrs had crossed, and another pass between the rocks and one of the hills; everywhere else rose walls of basalt.

The men cheered at the water. In the orange tint of the setting sun it was quenching the thirst of the saigas, the horses, the wild sheep with bearded faces, the asses with dainty hoofs, the deer more flighty than falling leaves. A brutal boar, quarrelsome and irritable, was the only one who drank with no fear. The others, their ears alert, their eyes darting, revealed the ceaseless watchfulness of the weak.

Suddenly all ears pricked up, all heads turned toward the stranger, and in rapid disorder horses, asses, saigas, sheep, and deer fled through the pass in the direction of the sunset. Only the boar remained, his little bloodshot eyes watching through their bristly lashes.

In the calm that followed the flight of the animals, the Oulhamrs drank and deliberated. It was too late to resume the route, and they had decided to take shelter when they heard a rumble in the distance.

"The aurochs!" Naoh cried.

He turned his head to the western pass and the three warriors listened. Then they lay down on the ground.

"It's not the aurochs," murmured Gaw.

And Naoh confirmed it: "They're mammoths!"

Quickly they examined the site: the river flowed between the basalt hill and a wall of red porphyry with a ledge wide enough for a huge animal to pass along. The Oulhamrs scaled this. Through the stone ravine water flowed in the eternal shade. Trees which had been felled by debris or uprooted by their own weight stretched horizontally across the abyss; others grew up out of the depths, slender and extremely long, expending all their vegetal energy to produce a few leaves in that place of faint light.

It was Naoh who first spotted a cave. It was hollowed in an irregular fashion, low and not very deep. The Oulhamrs did not go in right away. First they searched it thoroughly from the outside. At length Naoh went ahead of his companions, lowering his head and dilating his nostrils. He came upon bones with pieces of flesh, horns, and jawbones. These disclosed the presence of a terrible and powerful hunter; Naoh continued to sniff the air. "It's the gray bear's cave," he declared. "It has been empty for more than one moon."

Nam and Gaw were hardly familiar with this imposing beast, as the Oulhamrs prowled in territory common to tigers, lions, aurochs, even mammoths, where
the gray bear was rare. Naoh had encountered him on
long-distance expeditions. He was familiar with his
ferocity, blind like the rhinoceros's, his strength that
nearly equaled the giant lion's, his furious and unshakable courage. The cave was empty, either because the
bear had abandoned it or was somewhere else for a few
weeks or a season, or because of some mishap in crossing the river. The bear would probably not return that
night, Naoh was telling his companions, when an immense noise vibrated through the rocks and along the
river. The powerful voices of the aurochs, like lions'
roars, reverberated throughout the pass. Naoh listened
apprehensively, for man seldom hunted the aurochs.
The bulls had an agility and grew to a height and power which their descendants would not possess. They
were aware of their strength, and they had no fear of
large beasts.

The three Oulhamrs had hardly left the darkness of
the cave when another noise arose, cutting through the
first as an axe splits the flesh of a goat. This cry was not as
deep and rhythmic as that of the aurochs. Yet, though
weaker, it heralded the strongest creatures that walked
the face of the earth. In that time the mammoth moved
about invincible. His height chased away lions and tigers, discouraged the gray bear. For thousands of years
man would not measure himself against him, and the
rhinoceros alone, blind and stupid, dared to give fight.

The mammoth was supple, swift, tireless, able to climb mountains. He had a reasoning mind and a tenacious memory. He grasped, moved, and measured objects with his trunk, sweeping the ground with his huge tusks. He handled himself wisely on expeditions and was aware of his supremacy. Life was good for this red-blooded beast, who was undoubtedly cleverer than the elephants, debased by man's long victory over them.

It happened that the leaders of the aurochs and the mammoths approached the edge of the water at the same time. The mammoths intended to pass first as always, and this rule found no opposition from the aurochs. However, some of the aurochs were irritated, led on by bulls who were not very familiar with the mammoths but were used to other herbivores giving way to them.

The eight chief bulls were gigantic, the largest of them being the size of a rhinoceros. They were impatient and burning with thirst. Seeing that the mammoths wanted to pass first, they let out a long war cry, their muzzles raised and their throats swelling like bagpipes.

The mammoths trumpeted. They were five old males, their bodies like mounds and their feet like trees. Their tusks, ten feet long, could cut through an oak; their trunks looked like black pythons, their heads like rocks. They were armored in a skin that was thick like the bark of an elm. Behind them followed the long herd the color of clay.

Meanwhile, with their lively little eyes fixed on the bulls, the old mammoths blocked the route, peacefully,

imperturbably, as if in meditation. The eight heavy-eyed, humpbacked aurochs, with woolly, bearded heads, their horns arching in opposite directions, shook their thick manes laden with mud. The strongest among them lowered his thick forehead with his horns glinting. He rushed head on against the nearest mammoth. Hit on the shoulder, though he cushioned the blow with a lash of his trunk, the colossus fell to his knees. The aurochs had the advantage, and redoubled the attack with his sharp horns; all the mammoth could do was use his trunk clumsily. In this huge melee of muscles the aurochs employed frenzied daring. With the nape of his neck palpitating and his muzzle frothing, his movements were neat and sure. He would win if he could knock down his adversary and open his belly where the skin was less thick and the flesh more sensitive.

The mammoth was aware of this, and his perilous situation made him clear-headed. Just one bound would put him on his feet again, but for this the aurochs would have to slacken the attack.

At first the combat had taken the other males by surprise. The four mammoths and the seven bulls stood face to face in awesome expectation. None made a move to intervene; they all felt the same menace. The mammoths showed the first signs of impatience. The tallest, breathing heavily, shook his membranous ears like giant bats' wings and began to advance. Almost at the same time, the one who was fighting the bull dealt him a violent blow in the legs with his trunk. The aurochs staggered in his turn and the mammoth got to his feet. The huge beasts again found themselves face to face. The mammoth, driven by rage, raised his trunk and trumpeted the signal to attack. His curved tusks hurled the aurochs down, breaking his bones. Then, advancing from one side, the mammoth brought his trunk down again. With increasing rage he crushed his adversary's body, stamped upon the long entrails and broken ribs, covering himself with blood up to his chest. The ghastly agony of the vanquished was drowned out in a rumble of noises: the battle between the huge males had begun. The seven aurochs and four mammoths hurled themselves against each other in blind battle, their bodies melded in a formless swarming mass, an immense crush of flesh molded in pain and rage.

In the first shock of battle inferior numbers had given the mammoths a disadvantage. One was brought to the ground by three bulls; another was immobilized on the defensive. But the other two gained a quick victory. Hurling themselves together against their antagonists, they pierced, crushed, and tore them apart. They lost more time in stamping on their victims than they had put into beating them. Then when they became aware of their companions' peril, they charged: the three aurochs who were set upon destroying the colossus were taken by surprise. They were overwhelmed in a single mass. Two were crushed beneath the heavy feet, and the third got away. With him the bulls who were fighting still were taken along, and the aurochs experienced the contagion of terror. First came uneasiness as before a storm, silence, a strange immobility that seemed to spread throughout the multitude. Then, eyes darting aimlessly, hoofs trampling like a downpour of rain, a hurtling retreat that became a battle in the narrow pass, in which each beast was transformed into fleeing energy and panic-stricken projectiles, the strong knocking down the weak and the swift ones escaping over the others' backs, while everywhere bones were breaking like trees felled by a cyclone.

The mammoths did not think of pursuit: once more they had shown the measure of their power and they knew themselves to be the masters of the earth. They lined up on the bank of the watering place and began to drink so that the water level was lowered in the streams.

On the side of the hills a host of smaller animals, still terrified by the struggle, watched the mammoths drink. The Oulhamrs also watched, stupefied by one of nature's great events.

In the Cave

THE night was about a third over. The white moon gleamed through a cloud. Its rays played on the river, on the brooding rocks, and one by one it dissolved the shadows of the watering place. The mammoths had departed; nothing was seen except from time to time a prowling animal, or a solitary brown owl on its silently flapping wings. And Gaw, whose turn it was, stood guard at the entrance to the cave. He was tired; his thoughts were rare and fleeting, only aroused by sudden noises, growing smells or new ones, by the starts and falls of the wind. He was in a torpid state where things were growing dimmer except for the feeling of danger. The sudden flight of a saiga made him raise his head. It was then he noticed, across the river on the steep top of the hill, a massive silhouette that swayed as it walked. Its heavy yet supple limbs and solid head tapering at the jaw, and a certain strangely human appearance, indicated a bear. Gaw knew the cave-dwelling bear, huge and with a bulging head, which lived peacefully in its lair and its pasture land, a herbivore that hunger alone would induce to eat flesh. The bear coming toward him was not of this kind. Gaw was sure when he saw it silhouetted in the moonlight: the flat cranium was covered with fur. In its movement the Oulhamr recognized assurance and menace, the ferocity of the carnivore. It was the gray bear, the rival of the great felines.

Gaw recalled the legends brought back by men who had traveled on the highland. The gray bear kills aurochs and urus and can transport them more easily than the lion can carry an antelope. With one sweep of his claws he can open the chest and belly of a man; he can strangle a horse with his paws, stand up to lion and tiger. Old Goun believed that he yields only to the giant lion, the mammoth, and the rhinoceros.

The son of the Saiga did not feel the sudden terror that he would have on sighting a tiger. For his encounters with cave bears had taught him that they were mild and untroublesome. At first this recollection reassured him; but the speed of the beast impressed him more and

more as its silhouette came into focus, so that Gaw ran back to his leader.

He had only to touch his hand and the tall figure stood up in the darkness. "What does Gaw want?" asked Naoh, coming to the entrance of the cave.

The young warrior stretched his hand toward the hilltop; the leader's face showed consternation:

"The gray bear!"

He examined the cave. He had taken care to gather stones and branches; there were several stone blocks near by which could make access to the cave difficult. But Naoh was thinking of fleeing, and escape was only possible by way of the watering place. If this swift, tireless, and determined animal decided on pursuit, he would almost certainly catch the fugitives. Their sole resource would be to climb a tree, as the gray bear could not climb. On the other hand, he was capable of waiting an unlimited time, and in the area there were only trees with small branches.

Had the beast seen Gaw squatting, camouflaged, among the stone blocks and intent on not moving? Or was he the cave's occupant, coming back after a long journey? As Naoh wondered, the animal began the descent of the steep slope. When he was on surer ground he raised his head, sniffed the damp air, and broke into a trot. For an instant the warriors thought he was leaving. But he stopped in front of the spot where the ledge was accessible: all retreat became impracticable. Upstream the ledge was interrupted by a sheer drop. Downstream they would have to run for it right under the eyes of the bear. He would have time to cross the narrow river and block the fugitives' way. The only thing left was to wait for the animal to leave or attack the cave.

Naoh wakened Nam and the three of them got to work rolling blocks of stone.

After some hesitation the bear decided to cross the river; he reached the ledge and began to climb. Nam and Gaw shuddered; the instinctual awareness of human weakness choked them. Not even Naoh was calm. He knew the adversary, and he knew it would take him a short time to kill three men. His thick skin and granite-hard bones were nearly invulnerable to the javelin, axe, and spear.

Meanwhile the Oulhamrs finished piling up the stone blocks. Soon nothing was left but an opening to the right at about a man's height. When the bear got near, he shook his head with a growl and looked about, disconcerted. For if he had smelled the presence of men and heard the noise of their working, he had not expected to find that the lair where he had spent so many seasons was closed up. He showed no caution upon recognizing the odor of weak animals whom he expected to feed on, but he was perplexed. He stretched himself in the moonlight, feeling comfortable in his fur, showing his silvery breast and wagging his cone-shaped head. Then, because of his morose nature, he became irritated and let out a hoarse noise. Impatient, he stood upon his hind legs, like a huge and hairy man with legs too short and torso out of proportion, and leaned over toward the opening that was still free.

In the darkness Nam and Gaw held their axes ready. The son of the Leopard raised his club: they waited for the beast to stick his paws in so they could hack at them. Instead the huge head came first, with its padded forehead, slavering lips, and teeth like spear points. The axes struck, the club whirled about helplessly because of the stone protrusions at the opening. The bear growled and withdrew. He was not wounded: there wasn't a trace of blood on his muzzle. His jaws twitched and his eyes gleamed with fury at being attacked. All the same he didn't ignore the lesson, but changed his tactic. As a burrowing animal experienced in handling obstacles, he knew that it was sometimes better to pull them down rather than face a dangerous passage head on. So he touched the wall, then pushed it. It vibrated at his weight.

With increased effort the animal worked with his paws, shoulder, and head, sometimes hurling himself against the barricade or poking it with his shiny claws. Finding a weak spot, he broke through the wall and made it shake. He hurled all his effort on that spot, which was especially favorable since the men's arms were too short to reach it. Naoh and Gaw, acting as buttresses against the bear, succeeded in stopping the swaying, while Nam leaned over the opening and took aim at the bear's eye with his javelin.

Shortly the bear discovered that the weak point had become unshakable. This change in events stupefied and exasperated him. He stopped and sat down to consider the wall and to sniff it. He shook his head as if in disbelief. Finally he came back to the obstacle, hitting it with his paw and shoulder. Seeing that it still resisted, he lost patience and gave way to his own brutal nature.

The free opening hypnotized him. It appeared to be the only point that could be crossed. So he threw himself against it in fury. A shaft whistled in the air and struck him near the eyelid without slowing down his attack. All the impetus of the charge, the mass of his flesh with the blood coursing through it, impelled his energies: the wall crumbled.

Naoh and Gaw had rushed to the back of the cave. Nam found himself caught in the monstrous paws. He had no hope of defending himself; he was like an antelope caught by a giant panther or a horse struck down by a lion; arms outstretched and mouth gaping, in a dulled state he waited for death. But Naoh, who had been taken by surprise, recovered his fighting spirit. He threw away the axe, which he deemed useless, and took his knotty oaken club in both hands.

The beast saw him coming. He put off doing away with the weak prey that palpitated beneath him, and brought his strength to bear against the adversary, thundering down on him with paws and fangs while the Oulhamr brought down his club. The weapon struck first, hitting the bear on the jaw. One of its spikes hit a nostril. The blow, though it glanced sideways and was not very effective, was so painful that the beast buckled. The second blow bounded off his indestructible cranium. Already the immense beast had pulled

(34)

himself together and charged frantically, but the Oul-hamr had taken refuge in the shadows in front of a jut-ting rock. Just in time, he disappeared; the bear collided violently into the basalt. Naoh came from the side and with a war cry bashed the staggering beast along the spine with his club. Weakened by the impact against the rock, the bear swayed on his haunches, and Naoh crushed his nostrils, paws, and jaws while Nam and Gaw split open his chest with their axes.

When at last the hulk stopped panting, the three men looked at each other in silence. It was a great moment. Naoh was shown to be the most awesome of the Oul-hamrs, and of all men, for neither Faouhm, nor Hoo, the son of the Tiger, nor any of the warriors whom Goun the Dry-Bones could remember had ever slain a gray bear with his club. And the legend was etched in the young men's minds to transmit to future genera-tions and increase their hopes, if Nam, Gaw, and Naoh did not die in the quest for Fire.

CHAPTER FOUR

The Giant Lion and the Tigress

Two days elapsed. Naoh and his companions left the savanna behind, traveling ever southward. They were crossing the forest now. It seemed interminable, interspaced with islands of grass and stones, lakes, ponds, and gullies. It spread out slowly, with unexpected rises, sheltering hyena, boar, wolf, roebuck, elk, and wild sheep. The rhinoceros with his cutlass tusk and even the giant lion wandered there. There also roamed the mammoth, who left behind a trail marked by destruction more violent than that of flood or cyclone.

In this awesome territory the Oulhamrs found food in abundance. Knowing they were themselves the prey of flesh-eaters, they walked alertly in triangle formation in order to control the widest possible space. By day their keen senses could guard them from ambush, but their most dangerous enemies only hunted in the dark.

The Oulhamrs chose with care their places of shelter; they halted long before nightfall. Often they took refuge in a hollow. At other times they relied on rocks, or else sheltered in deep thickets or among densely growing trees.

More than anything else, the lack of Fire made them suffer. On nights when there was no moon, it seemed to them that they had entered the darkness forever. It weighed them down and engulfed them. Each evening they watched the underbrush as if they expected the flames to spark in their cage and swell to devour the dead branches. But all they saw were the lost sparks of the stars or the eyes of a beast. Their weakness and the immensity of their surroundings crushed their spirits.

After a few days, finally the forest opened up. Woods still filled the west, but in the east a plain stretched out, part savanna and part brush with a few islands of trees. A river flowed to the east, banked with black poplar, ash, aspen, alder, rushes, and reeds. Stones lay about at random in reddish masses. And although it was still broad daylight, long shadows darkened the sun's rays.

The three men considered the terrain with misgivings: many animals would cross the plain to the bank of the river when darkness came on. So they made haste to drink, and then explored the site. But they found that the stones were too small and too scattered to use for building a shelter. They were ready to go back to the forest when Nam noticed, not far from the bank, some enormous boulders very close together, two of which touched at the top; it made a cavity with four openings. The first three would let in animals smaller than men — wolves, dogs, or panthers. The fourth would allow a tall warrior to pass, provided he lay flat on the ground. It would not be passable for bears, lions, or tigers.

At a signal from their companion, Naoh and Gaw ran up. They were afraid at first that they would not be able to squeeze into the refuge. But by lying on the ground and twisting his head, Naoh got in with no effort. In this way, they found themselves safer shelter than any hitherto, for the stone blocks were so heavy and so tightly jammed that a herd of mammoths couldn't have torn them apart. There was space as well, for ten men could have easily fitted in.

The prospect of a perfect night overjoyed the Oulhamrs. For the first time since their departure they could laugh at the threat of animals.

They ate the raw flesh of a fawn they had killed in the morning, with nuts they had gathered in the forest. Then they sat outside the shelter, looking over the countryside. A few elk and deer were making for the water. Crows flew up with a war cry; an eagle glided at the level of the clouds. Then a lynx bounded in pur-

(38)

suit of a teal, and a leopard slunk furtively among the willows.

Suddenly the three men lifted their heads, their senses heightened by peril. Their hesitation was momentary: at a sign from Naoh, Nam and Gaw slipped under the sheltering rocks. He followed them himself at the moment a giant stag sprang from the forest. The beast was in precipitous flight. His head with its great web of horn was thrown back, a foam mixed with crimson flowed from the nostrils, the hooves surged like branches in a cyclone. The stag had made thirty bounds when the enemy leaped into view. It was a tiger with stocky limbs and a limber spine, who covered twenty yards with each move. His flexible leaps seemed like gliding in air. Each time the feline reached the ground there was a brief pause and a reconcentration of energy.

In the stag's less ample movements there wasn't a pause. Each jump was the accelerated succession of the one before. At this point in the pursuit he was losing ground. For the tiger the race had just begun, whereas the deer had come from a distance.

"The tiger will catch the great stag," said Nam in a trembling voice.

Naoh, watching the chase with fascination, replied, "The giant stag is tireless!"

Not far from the river the stag's speed was halved. With a tremendous effort he sped up again. The two bodies hurled themselves on with equal speed, then the leaps of the tiger got smaller. Undoubtedly he would have given up the chase if the river had not been close; he hoped to gain ground by swimming, for which his body was well made. When he got to the riverbank and plunged into the water, the stag was thirty yards ahead. The tiger dashed into the stream with amazing velocity, and the stag advanced at a barely slower rate. This was the moment of life or death. As the river was not wide the stag still could land with a lead. If he hesitated climbing the bank he would be caught. He knew it, but risked making a detour to choose a landing point: this was a pebbly little promontory with a gradual slope. The stag had calculated right; after a slight hesitation he climbed out ten yards ahead of the tiger. On landing, the tiger's paws got tangled; he stumbled and somersaulted: the stag was in the clear. There was nothing for the tiger to do but halt the pursuit. He crossed the river again and stretched out his body on the bank.

Suddenly the carnivore leaped to his feet. His paws stiffened as with his great yellow, staring, almost haggard eyes he watched a monster animal advance from the forest. It looked like a tiger, but taller and more compact; its mane was a lion's, and its deep chest and sedate pace. Although it advanced without pause, aware of its supremacy, it showed the hesitation of animals that are not on their own hunting ground. But the tiger was. For ten seasons he had held sway over the territory, and the other beasts, leopard, panther, and hyena, had lived in the shadow of him. He had only to choose the prey and it was his. No creature stood up to the tiger when, on a chance encounter, he slaughtered elk, buck, stag, urus, aurochs, or antelope. Only the crossing of an invulnerable rhinoceros made him stand aside, or that of a mammoth with his massive feet, for he judged it too difficult to fight them. The kind of animal which had just appeared was unknown to him, and he was astonished.

It was a very rare animal of ancient origins, a species which had been dying out for thousands of years. All his instincts told the tiger that it was stronger, better armed, and faster than himself, but his long experience of victory made him revolt against his fear. As the enemy approached he moved aside rather than retreated; his manner remained threatening. When the distance between them was sufficiently shortened the lion-tiger swelled his huge chest and roared. Then, gathering his forces, he sprang in attack, covering thirty feet. The tiger drew back and turned to beat a retreat. Then his rage made him wheel around again and accept the combat, his eyes gleaming.

Suddenly he was no longer by himself. A tigress had just appeared on the grassland, and came running up to the defense of her mate.

The giant lion hesitated, doubtful of his strength. Perhaps he would have withdrawn at that point and left the tigers to their territory had not his adversary, excited by the mewing of the approaching tigress, shown signs of attacking. The enormous feline could resign himself to yielding place, but the recollection of all the flesh he had torn apart and the limbs he had crushed forced him to punish aggression. The distance between him and the tiger was a single leap. He covered it without hitting his mark, as the other had veered and was attempting to attack on the flank. The lion stopped to meet the assault. Claws and fangs interlocked with a clattering and hoarse breathing. The tiger, being shorter, tried to get his enemy by the throat. He nearly succeeded, but was thrown off by able movements. He found himself laid out under a crushing paw, and the giant lion proceeded to rip open his belly. The entrails gushed out like blue creepers, the scarlet blood spilled over the grass, and a terrible howl made the savanna tremble. Then the tigress approached. Hesitantly she sniffed the warm flesh, taking in the defeat of her male, and let out a wail for help.

At this the tiger got up with a final warlike impulse, but he was entangled in his own entrails and held motionless, his limbs failing, though his eyes were still full of life. Instinctively the tigress gauged the energy remaining to the creature who had shared the prey with her, watched over her cubs, protecting their kind against countless traps. Now she was aware that something more terrible than tigers stood before her and so, quivering with the will to live, with a hollow groan and a long glance behind her she turned tail and made for the forest.

The giant lion made no move to follow her; he was reveling in his supremacy. The tiger no longer worried him; nevertheless he kept an eye on it, hesitating to finish it off, for he had the prudent temperament of a

conqueror, who fears to receive wounds needlessly.

The red glow of evening came on, filtering through the forest depths; the animals of the day grew still. As the sun sank behind a sea of cliffs, the great moon rose in the east.

No other creature was to be seen but the two beasts. In the shadows a multitude of animals could smell their menacing presence. The giant lion once again sensed his failing strength. The numberless prey were teeming in the thickets and clearings, and yet he feared hunger every day. For he carried his scent with him. It gave him away more surely than his step, the crunch of the earth, grass, leaves, and branches; it was the terror and the means of safety of the weak. Suddenly everything fled into hiding and the land was deserted. The feline seemed to be alone in the world.

As the night was drawing on, the great beast became hungry. He had been driven from his territory by a flood, and since then he had crossed many rivers and roamed unfamiliar lands. Now that he had conquered the tiger his nostrils flared, seeking other scents in the wind. Then hunger made him turn back to the warm innards of the defeated animal. He sniffed them but was repelled as by poison. Impatiently he leaped on the tiger and finished it off. Then he began to prowl.

The profile of the jagged stones attracted him. His sense of smell was not equal to the wolves', and since the stones were against the wind he had been unaware of the men's presence. Approaching, he realized there was prey and began hopefully to sniff the air.

The Oulhamrs shivered as they watched the huge silhouette. In the sunset they saw the lion-tiger circling about their refuge; he poked his muzzle into the cracks; his eyes flashed like violet stars; everything about him spoke of haste and hunger. When he got to the opening the men had slipped through, he tried to stick his head and shoulders in, making the Oulhamrs wonder if the rocks were stable. With each movement of the heavy animal, Nam and Gaw huddled together gasping with fear. Filled with hatred at being stalked, Naoh pitted his intelligence against the beast's ancient instinct and strength. His anger grew as the beast started to scratch the earth. Although the giant lion was not a burrowing animal, he knew how to enlarge an opening or overturn an obstacle. His effort threw the men into consternation, prompting Naoh to squat down and strike out with his spear: he hit the beast's head, making him let out a furious roar and stop digging. The lion's eyes searched the darkness and clearly made out the three silhouettes.

He resumed his prowling, trying all the exits, always coming back to the larger one. At length he began to dig again: another blow from the spear interrupted his labor and made him retreat, this time with less surprise. In his thick mind he knew that to get into the lair was impossible, yet he wouldn't abandon the prey, hoping that what was so close would not escape. After one last look at the men he seemed to ignore their existence, and took off for the forest.

The three Oulhamrs were exultant; their haven

seemed even safer than before. They thought the giant lion would surely return, but as they had no very precise consciousness of time, they enjoyed the fullness of the present moment; the period separating the evening twilight from the dawn seemed inexhaustible.

As was his custom, Naoh had taken the first watch. He wasn't sleepy. Excited by the fight between the tiger and the giant lion, he was conscious of all the ideas accumulated from tradition and experience turning about in his mind. They combined confusedly to form his conception of the world. And already the world was vast in the Oulhamrs' intelligence. They knew the path of the sun and the moon; the cycles of darkness following light and light succeeding darkness, of the cold season alternating with the hot; the routes of streams and rivers; birth, old age, and the death of men; the form, habits, and strength of the numberless beasts; the growth of trees and plants; the art of fashioning the spear, axe, club, knife, and javelin and how to handle them; the movement of wind and clouds, capricious rain, and wild thunder. Finally, they knew of Fire — the most terrible and the gentlest of living things, strong enough to destroy a whole savanna and forest with their rhinoceroses, lions, tigers, bears, aurochs, and and uruses.

The life of Fire had always fascinated Naoh. Like the beasts it has to have prey: it feeds on branches, dry grass, grease. It grows. Each fire is born of other fires, each fire can die. But the stature of a fire is unlimited, and on the other hand it can be cut in two endlessly

(46)

and each piece will live. It decreases when deprived of food, making itself as small as a fly, yet it can come alive again along a blade of grass to become as vast as a swamp. It is an animal and it is not an animal. It has neither paws nor crawling body, yet it outstrips antelopes; no wings, yet it flies in the clouds; no mouth, yet it breathes, growls, roars; no hands or claws, yet it takes possession of wide expanses. Naoh loved, hated, and revered it. As a child he had sometimes felt its bite. He knew it made no distinctions of person, ready to devour those who sustained it, more deceitful than the hyena, more ferocious than the panther. But its presence was a delight; it dispelled the cruelty of cold nights, gave repose to the exhausted, and made man's weakness imposing.

In the dim light of the basalt rocks Naoh saw in his mind's eye the camp bonfire and the glimmer that played on Gammla's features.

The moon was halfway to the zenith when Gaw took the watch for Naoh, who was drowsy. Vaguely in the background the river could be heard flowing in the vast silence. Then menacing sounds returned, roars in the underbrush, twigs snapping in the bushes, hyenas and wolves together sending up howls from their bloody jaws. Gaw poked his head out of the stone shelter and using sight, hearing, and smell, searched the terrain. An agonized cry, a short growl, then the branches parted. The giant lion came out of the forest carrying a deer between his jaws. Beside him, still humble but already familiar, the tigress crept like a gigantic reptile. Both headed for the men's refuge.

Filled with fear, Gaw touched Naoh's shoulder. The men watched the two beasts a long time. The lion was tearing apart his prey, and the tigress watched the killer of her mate out of the corner of her eye, sometimes shying away with sudden fear and uncertainty. And Naoh felt a terrible apprehension grip his chest and stifle his breathing.

CHAPTER FIVE

In the Stone Shelter

WHEN the morning trailed across the earth the giant lion and the tigress were still there. They were asleep near the deer carcass in the pale rays of sunlight. And the three men, safe in their stone refuge, could not take their eyes off them.

Naoh thought that the memory of blows from the spear had drawn the giant lion back to the rocks; he regretted that useless action. For the Oulhamr had no doubt that the beasts could communicate with each other and that each one would take a turn watching beside the shelter. Stories crossed his mind about the rancor and tenacity of animals that had been offended by men. Sometimes his anger got the better of him; he got up and brandished his club or axe. But the anger was quickly stilled: despite his victory over the gray bear, he estimated that a man was no match for the great carnivores. The trickery that had succeeded in the darkness of the cave would not be effective against the giant lion or the tigress. He saw no alternative to combat: either they would die of hunger in the stone shelter or they would have to take advantage of a moment when the tigress was alone. But would he be able to count altogether on Nam and Gaw? He shook himself as if he were cold; he saw the eyes of his companions fixed on him. He felt the need of reassuring them: "Nam and Gaw have escaped from the jaws of a bear; they will escape the claws of the giant lion!"

The two young Oulhamrs turned their faces toward the sleeping animals. Naoh replied to their thoughts: "The giant lion and the tigress won't always be together. Hunger will separate them. When the lion is in the forest we will fight, but Nam and Gaw will have to obey my commands." The son of the Poplar, who was quicker to express himself, cried, "Nam will obey to the death!" The other raised his two arms: "With Naoh, Gaw fears nothing!"

The leader looked at them kindly; it was as if the energy of life itself had infused them, and with a wave of feelings which they had no words to express, Nam and Gaw brandished their axes, letting out war cries.

At the sound, the felines started: the Oulhamrs yelled louder, signaling defiance; the beasts growled angrily. Then calm returned. The three men waited, possessing the same patience as the beasts. Nam and Gaw dozed off at intervals. Naoh ruminated on vague and monotonous projects like those of the mammoths, wolves, or dogs. They still had enough meat for a meal, but thirst was beginning to torment them: still, it would not become intolerable for a while.

Toward evening the giant lion stood up. Darting an angry glance at the stone blocks, he assured himself of the enemy's presence, and began to circle about in front of the gaps in the shelter. At length, remembering that the fortified spot could not be entered and that sharp claws sprang out from it, he stopped prowling and lay down near the deer carcass. The tigress was there before him. They made short work of what was left, and then the huge lion turned his reddish head toward the tigress. A kind of tenderness emanated from the wild beast to which the tigress responded with a mewing, her long body stretched out on the grass. The lion-tiger rubbed his muzzle against the spine of his companion and licked her with his rough and flexible tongue. She yielded to his caress with half-open eyes, then she stepped back menacingly. The male growled, a subdued and coaxing growl, while the tigress played about in the evening light. The orange streaks of light made her look like a dancing flame; she flattened herself out like a huge snake, crawled into the grass, and hid, then took off again with great leaps. Her companion stood still and taut at first, his eyes gleaming red in the sun, then he rushed upon her. She dashed off, slipping into a grove of ash trees, and he slunk after her. When Nam saw them disappear, he said, "They've left: we must cross the river." "Doesn't Nam have any ears or smell?" said Naoh. "Or does he think he can leap faster than the giant lion?"

Nam lowered his head: a cavernous growl arose near the ash trees which gave significance to Naoh's words. The warrior understood the peril was as close as when the carnivores were sleeping in front of the basalt rocks. Nevertheless, some hope remained to the Oulhamrs: because of their union, the lion-tiger and the tigress would all the more feel the need of a lair, for the great beasts rarely lodge on the bare earth, especially in the rainy season.

When their enemies reappeared, the giant lion's pace was solemn and heavy; the tigress circled about him with tremendous gaiety. They came back to sniff the presence of the men just as the sun sank, when an immense shiver came across the land and hungry animals raised their voices; the monstrous jaws kept passing back and forth in front of the Oulhamrs, eyes of fire dancing like gleams in a swamp. At length the lion crouched while his companion slunk off into the grass.

The moon lit up the tigress, who prowled the savanna and the forest looking for prey. Her movements worried Naoh, but the tigress finally went so far afield that they could have given battle to her companion. If Nam and Gaw's strength had been comparable to his own, Naoh could have risked the offensive. He suffered from thirst, while Nam suffered even more; even though it was not his turn to watch he could not sleep. In the dark, the feverish eyes of the young Oulhamr were open; Naoh himself was dejected. Never before had he felt the distance so great that separated him from the band.

He dreamed on and slept lightly enough to be wakened by the least approach. Time passed beneath the stars. Naoh only awoke on the return of the tigress. She brought back no prey but seemed exhausted. The lion-tiger had gotten up, sniffed her a long time, and gone off to hunt in his turn. He also followed along the edge of the river, crouched in the bushes, and pushed on into the forest. Naoh was engrossed in watching him. He often had to wake the others (Nam had succumbed to sleep), but a sure instinct warned him that the brute was not far enough away yet. Finally he made his decision; he touched his companions on the shoulder, and as soon as they were on their feet he whispered, "Are Nam and Gaw ready to fight?"

They answered, "The son of the Saiga will follow Naoh!" "Nam will fight with spear and axe!"

The young warriors considered the tigress. Although the beast was still lying down, she was by no means asleep; at some distance, with her back turned to the basalt blocks, she watched. Now Naoh during his watch had silently cleared the exit. If the attention of the tigress was caught immediately, a single man, two

(53)

at the most, would have time to dash from the shelter. Having made sure that the weapons were in good shape, Naoh began by advancing his spear and club, then he slipped out with great care. Luck was with them: the howls of wolves and the calls of a screech owl covered the slight noise of their bodies brushing the earth. Naoh made it to the prairie and already Gaw's head was coming through the opening. The young warrior came out with a brusque movement; the tigress turned around and stared fixedly at the two men. Surprised, she did not attack at once, so that Nam could come out in his turn. Then the tigress made a single bound with a mew for help; she continued to come closer to the men without haste, sure that they could not escape. Meanwhile, they had raised their spears. Nam must hurl his first, then Gaw, and both should aim at the paws. The son of the Poplar took advantage of a good range. The weapon whistled through the air, hitting too high, close to the shoulder. Whether it was that the distance was too great or that the point had struck on a bias, the tigress seemed not to feel any pain; she growled and sped up. In his turn, Gaw hurled his weapon. He missed the beast, who had shied to the side. It was Naoh's turn. Stronger than his companions, he could inflict a deep wound. He hurled the spear when the tigress was only twenty paces away and hit her in the nape. The wound did not stop the beast, whose speed increased.

She hit the three men like a boulder: Gaw was downed by the blow of claws on his chest. But the

heavy club of Naoh had struck; the tigress howled with a broken paw while the son of the Poplar attacked with his spear. She swerved at prodigious speed, flattened Nam on the ground, and stood up on her hind paws to reach Naoh. The monstrous jaws were upon him, and her burning fetid breath; a claw tore at him, but his club struck again. Howling with pain, the beast was dizzied, permitting the man to get free and bash a second foot. The tigress wheeled upon herself, trying to get her balance; she slashed at the air while the club struck relentlessly at her limbs. The animal fell, all her paws broken, and Naoh could have disposed of her, but his companions' wound worried him. He found Gaw standing, his torso red with spurting blood, three long wounds streaking his flesh. As for Nam, he lay stunned, with wounds that seemed light. A deep pain spread in his chest and loins; he could not get up. To Naoh's questions, he answered like someone half asleep. Then the leader asked, "Can Gaw make it to the river?"

"Gaw will go to the river," murmured the young Oulhamr.

Naoh lay down and pressed his ear to the ground, then he took a long breath. Nothing revealed the approach of the giant lion, and since after the turmoil of combat thirst had become intolerable, the leader lifted Nam in his arms and carried him to the water. There he helped Gaw quench his thirst, drank abundantly himself, and gave Nam to drink by pouring the water between his lips from the hollow of his hands. Afterwards he headed back to the basalt rocks with

Nam on his shoulder, supporting Gaw, who staggered. The Oulhamrs hardly knew how to treat wounds: they covered them with a few leaves, choosing aromatic ones from an instinct more animal than human. Naoh went out to look for willow and mint leaves, which he crushed and applied to Gaw's chest. The blood was flowing less freely, and it looked as if the wounds were not fatal. Nam came out of his stupor but his limbs remained motionless. Naoh did not forget to speak encouragement: "Nam and Gaw fought well — the sons of Oulhamr will proclaim their courage."

The young warriors' faces lit up with the joy of seeing their leader again victorious. "Naoh defeated the tigress," murmured the son of the Saiga in a hoarse voice, "as he had conquered the gray bear!"

"There is no warrior as strong as Naoh!" Nam exclaimed.

Then the son of the Leopard repeated the words of hope so forcefully that the wounded men felt confidence in the future: "We shall bring back Fire!" and he added, "The giant lion is still far away: Naoh will look for game."

Naoh moved back and forth across the plain, mostly close to the river. Now and then he paused before the tigress, who was alive but unable to move. Her eyes gleamed in spite of her bleeding flesh: she watched the tall warrior moving around her. The wounds on flank and back were light but her paws would take a long time healing.

Naoh stopped close to the defeated prey; attributing

human feelings to her, he cried, "Naoh has broken the tigress's paws: he has made her weaker than a mother wolf." At the warrior's approach she tried to raise herself with an angry, frightened growl. He lifted his club: "Naoh could kill the tigress and she could not raise a single claw to fight him."

A distant noise was heard. Naoh crept up in the tall grass. Does appeared, running from wolves that could not be seen yet but whose howls were audible. They dashed into the water upon catching the scent of the tigress and of the man, but Naoh's javelin whistled through the air. One of the does turned aside, hit in the flank. Naoh swam several strokes and caught her. He finished her with a blow of the club, hiked her onto his shoulders, and carried her on the run to the shelter as he smelled the approach of danger. As he slipped through the rocks, the giant lion came out of the forest.

CHAPTER SIX

Escape in the Night

THE next day Naoh saw that Gaw's wounds were healing, but the warrior was still unable to regain the strength that had ebbed away with his blood. As for Nam, although he was no longer in pain, one of his legs still remained useless. Naoh was consumed by impatience and worry.

That night the giant lion roamed farther off as the beasts grew more aware of him. His presence filled the dark shadows of the forest and shot fear along the riverbank. The lion had a bitter task, since he was himself insatiable and he had to feed the tigress. They both endured hunger; their life was more desperate and miserable than that of the wolves.

During the absence of the giant lion, Naoh went to the river; Gaw dragged along after him. When they had quenched their thirst, they took back water for Nam in a piece of hollowed bark.

By the second day Nam and Gaw felt themselves strong enough to cross the stretch of water, and Naoh set the time of their escape for that night. All afternoon the lion-tiger showed signs of anxiousness. He came out of his sleep shivering: Naoh surmised that without doubt that night, when the lion went off to hunt, he would look for a lair as well. His absence would be prolonged.

Night came upon them heavy and humid. The chalk-red sunset stretched across the sky for a long time; the grass and the trees bent beneath a downpour of rain and the leaves fell to the ground with a sound like feeble rustle of wings or the buzz of insects. The Oulhamrs would have time to cross the river; the rain would help them in their retreat; it would soak the ground and wipe out the odor of their traces, which the giant lion would not follow with any acuteness.

Sometime after twilight the giant cat began to prowl. First he explored the neighboring territory, assuring himself that there was no prey close at hand, and then, as on other evenings, he penetrated deep into the forest. Naoh waited uncertainly, because the odor from the humid vegetation did not permit the scent of the beasts to become easily apparent. The noise of the leaves and the falling rain confused his hearing as well. At last he gave the signal, taking the lead in the expedition, while Nam and Gaw followed on his right and left.

First they must cross the river. During his expeditions Naoh had discovered a fordable point just to the middle of the current. From there they would have to swim toward a boulder, where the ford resumed. Before setting out to cross the river, the warriors covered their tracks. They made several feints for a while close by the water, doubling back on themselves and then resuming their direction, stopping short and stamping in order to emphasize the trace of their movements. They swam for the ford rather than approaching it directly.

Once across, they resumed the maneuver of crisscrossing their path, executing great twists and arbitrary curves. When they had covered several hundred yards of ground they considered that enough had been done to throw off their pursuer, and they continued the journey straight ahead. They advanced for a while in silence, then Nam and Gaw called to one another while Naoh pricked up his ears. In the distance the roar had cut through the air. Three times it was repeated, followed by a long-drawn-out mewing.

Nam cried, "It's the giant lion!"

"Let's walk faster," muttered Naoh.

They went on a few hundred feet without any noise. Then the beast's voice reverberated from closer by. Again they increased their speed, while the roars continued, abrupt, strident, full of rage and frustration. They understood that the beast was running about after their muddled traces; their hearts pounded in their chests like a pickaxe against a tree trunk. They felt naked and defenseless before the crushing mass of the dark. The giant lion could only follow by the trail they left, and if he crossed the river he would find himself up against the men's ruse and would not be able to discover what direction they had taken.

A tremendous roar split the air. Nam and Gaw drew closer to Naoh. "The giant lion has crossed the water," Gaw murmured.

"Keep going!" commanded their leader, while at the same time he stopped and lay on the ground in order to catch the sound's reverberations.

New noises burst upon each other.

Standing up, Naoh cried, "The giant lion is still on the other side of the river."

The howling voice grew fainter. The beast had abandoned pursuit and was withdrawing to the north.

They walked on for a long while. The downpour had turned to a drizzle, but the shadows remained deep. A thick wall of clouds masked the stars. All they could see was the ephemeral glow of phosphorus which plants give off and which hovers on the surface of water.

Nam and Gaw began to tire. Nam felt his bones weakening, and Gaw's wounds had begun to smart; it was time to look for shelter. Still, they covered several more miles. The air became more humid again; the wind rose over the open stretches. They guessed that a large body of water was close by, and soon their expectation was confirmed.

Everything seemed at peace. The slightest of noises indicated the flight of an animal; a form would appear and disappear again in a rapid bound. Naoh at last selected an immense black poplar for their shelter. The tree could offer no defense against the attack of a beast, but how to find a sure refuge in the dark, or one that was not occupied? The moss was damp and the air sharp. It mattered little to the Oulhamrs; their skin was as resistant to the elements as the hide of bears or boars. Nam and Gaw stretched out on the ground and instantly went off to sleep; Naoh stood watch. He was not tired; he had taken a long rest beneath the basalt rocks and, well conditioned to marches, to labors, and to fighting, he steeled himself to extend his watch so that Nam and Gaw might build up their strength.

◄◄ Part Two ►►

CHAPTER ONE

The Ashes

For a long time they remained in the darkness that had slowed up their escape. Then light filtered through in the east. Spreading softly amid the mossy clouds, it came down like a cloth of pearls. Naoh saw that a lake, of which he couldn't see the end, obstructed the southern route. The lake rippled slowly. The Oulhamrs wondered if they should go around it to the east where a range of hills could be seen, or toward the west, which was pale and flat terrain dotted with trees.

The light remained weak. A soft breeze from the

land played on the water. High up the wind rose, parting the clouds and blowing them about. The outline of the moon in its last quarter showed through the raveled clouds, then against the blue expanse of the sky. To the sharp eye of Naoh the lay of the land was visible to the frontier of the horizon. To the east he discerned hillsides with their tree-lines etched against the moonlight, which showed the direction their journey was to take; to the south and west the lake stretched indefinitely.

Silence reigned, seeming to spread from the water up to the silvery crescent in the sky. The wind grew so weak that it barely sighed in the leaves.

Tired of standing motionless and impatient to get a clear view, Naoh left the shade of the poplar and prowled along the riverbank. According to the formation of land and vegetation, the site opened up or narrowed, the eastern extremes of the lake becoming clearer. Numerous tracks indicated the passage of herds and beasts of prey.

Suddenly, with a shudder, the Oulhamr stopped. His eyes narrowed and his nostrils flared, while his heart beat with anxiety and strange fascination. Memories crowded in upon him with such force that he imagined he could see the Oulhamr camp, the smoking fire, and the supple figure of Gammla. For there in the green grass was a hollowed place with embers and half-consumed branches; the wind had not yet dispersed the white powder of the ashes.

Naoh imagined the relaxation of a halt, the aroma of

(68)

meat being roasted, the tender warmth and ruddy flickering of the flames. But at the same time, in his mind he saw the enemy.

Fearful and prudent, he knelt down to examine the traces of the dangerous wanderers. Shortly he calculated that there were at least two times as many warriors as the fingers on his two hands, and no women, old men, or children. It was a forage and reconnaissance expedition which bands sometimes sent out at great distances. The state of the bones and meat fibers confirmed the evidence he drew from the grass.

Naoh needed to know where the hunters came from and what direction they had taken. He feared they belonged to the race of man-eaters, the Kzams, who since Goun's youth had occupied the southern territories on either side of the Great River. The height of this race exceeded that of the Oulhamrs and of all other races that had been seen by the chiefs and the old men. They alone fed on the flesh of their own kind, though they did not prefer it to the flesh of elk, boar, fallow deer, roebuck, horse, or wild ass. Their population did not seem large: only three bands were known of, whereas Ouag, the greatest traveler born among the Oulhamrs, had encountered everywhere peoples that did not eat the flesh of men.

As memories kept coming to Naoh, he did not stop following the tracks. The task was easy, as the wanderers, confident of their numbers, disdained to cover their traces. They had circled the lake to the east and

were probably trying to regain the banks of the Great River.

Two plans offered themselves to Naoh: to catch up with the expedition before they reached their hunting grounds and make off with the Fire by trickery; or else to get ahead of them to their band, which was without its best warriors, and look for a favorable opportunity. In their youthful impatience, the three men decided on the first plan.

So as not to take the wrong road they must first follow the trail. Naoh's savage imagination, sweeping across water, hills, and steppes, kept seeing the roaming warriors who carried with them men's supreme weapon. His reverie had the precision of reality. For a long time the watcher gave himself up to it, while the wind calmed down, grew weak, and ceased from leaf to leaf, from one blade of grass to the next.

CHAPTER TWO

The Lookout by the Fire

For two days the Oulhamrs had been following the trail of the man-eaters. First they circled the lake to the foot of the hills; then they came into land where trees alternated with grasslands. Their task was easy because the travelers were advancing nonchalantly, lighting big fires to roast their prey and shelter themselves from the cold, foggy nights.

On the other hand, Naoh constantly used tricks to fool anyone who might be following. He chose hard ground, or supple grass which quickly snapped back;

he took advantage of stream beds, forded or swam across certain turns in the lake, and sometimes crisscrossed his tracks. Despite these precautions he gained ground. On the second day he was so close to the enemy camp that he believed they could reach it in one night's march.

"Nam and Gaw must get their weapons ready and have courage," he said. "Tonight they will see Fire again!"

The young warriors were excited at the prospect of seeing the leaping flames, while they were frightened at the thought of the enemy's strength.

"First let's rest," continued the son of the Leopard. "We will sneak up on them while they are asleep and try to take the watchers by surprise."

Nam and Gaw felt the presence of a greater peril than all the others, for the legend of the Kzams was formidable. Their strength, bravery, and ferocity exceeded that of all known men. Sometimes the Oulhamrs had taken small groups of them by surprise and wiped them out: more often, it had been the Oulhamrs who had perished under the slashing axes and clubs of the Kzams. According to old Goun, they were descended from the gray bear; their arms were longer than other men's, their bodies as hairy as those of Aghoo and his brothers. And because they fed on the bodies of their enemies, they frightened more timid peoples. When the son of the Leopard had spoken, Nam and Gaw bowed their heads, trembling; then they rested till the middle of the night.

They got up before the light of the crescent moon whitened the sky. Naoh had identified the trail beforehand, and they marched at first in darkness. At the rising of the moon, they realized that they had gotten sidetracked; then they recovered the trail. They pushed their way through underbrush, skirted some swampland, and crossed a river. At last, from the top of a hillock, hidden amid scrubby grass, with terrific emotion they saw the Fire. Nam and Gaw shivered; Naoh remained squatting motionless and breathing heavily. After so many nights spent in the cold, the rain and darkness, with so many things to fight — hunger, thirst, the bear, the tigress, the giant lion — it was before them at last, the brilliant sign of Man.

It was not far from a pond, on a plain dotted with turpentine trees and sycamores, a semicircular bonfire whose flames flickered languidly over the logs. It threw out a twilight glow which permeated and enlivened everything around it.

The men were sleeping, covered with skins of elk, wolves, mountain goats. Their axes, clubs, and javelins were scattered about on the ground; two warriors were watching. One of them, seated on a pile of dry wood, his shoulders covered with a goatskin, had his hand on his spear. A ray of light played on his face, which was covered up to the eyes with hair like a fox's. His hairy hide resembled a mountain goat's. He had a flat nose with circular nostrils; the weight of his long arms hunched his shoulders, and his legs were short, thick, and bowed. The other watcher walked furtively around

(74)

the fire. He stopped at intervals, pricked an ear, and sniffed the damp air which sank to the plain as the hot vapors rose up from the fire. His height was equal to Naoh's, his head enormous with ears like a wolf, pointed and retractile. His hair and beard grew in tufts between spots of saffron-colored skin. The three Oulhamrs could see his eyes glittering in the half-light or gleaming blood-red in the reflection of the flames. He had pectoral muscles flexed above a flat stomach, triangle-shaped thighs, shins like the head of an axe, and feet that would have been short but for the length of the toes. The whole body, heavy and jointed like a buffalo's, displayed an immense strength but less capacity for speed than the bodies of the Oulhamrs.

The watcher had interrupted his course; he turned his head in the direction of the hill. Doubtless a vague scent bothered him, in which he recognized neither the smell of animals nor that of his own people. The other watchman, with less acute nostrils, dozed on.

"We are too close," Gaw remarked softly. "The wind carries our scent to them."

Naoh nodded his head, for he was much more afraid of the enemy's power of smell than of his sight or hearing. "We must go against the wind!" Nam added. "The wind is following the trail of the Kzams," Naoh replied. "If we turn, they will be walking behind us." He did not need to explain his thoughts: Nam and Gaw understood as well as the beasts the necessity of following, not preceding, prey except to ambush them. Meanwhile, the watcher spoke to his companion, who shook his head. He seemed about to sit down in turn, but he changed his mind and walked in the direction of the hill.

"We must retreat!" said Naoh. He looked for a shelter which would obstruct their scent. A thick bush grew close to the summit; the Oulhamrs concealed themselves in it, and as the wind was light it did not penetrate, but carried an odor that was too weak for human nostrils. Shortly, the watcher stopped; after taking several deep breaths he returned to camp. The Oulhamrs remained motionless for a long time. The son of the Leopard sought out strategies with his eyes in the dimmed glow of the bonfire, but he came up with nothing. For if the slightest obstacle can deceive sharp eyesight and if it is possible to walk softly enough on the steppe to fool antelope or elk, still an odor is given off when a man passes and it remains on his track; only distance or a counter-blowing wind can hide it. The yelping of a jackal made Naoh lift his head. He listened to it in silence at first, then he let out a short laugh. "We are now in the country of jackals," he said. "Let Nam and Gaw try to kill one."

His companions looked at him in astonishment. He continued: "Naoh will keep watch in this bush. The jackal is as tricky as a wolf; a man could never approach him. But he is always hungry. Nam and Gaw must put down a piece of flesh and wait at a short distance. When the jackal comes, your spear must be quicker than he is."

Jackals are not difficult to follow; their voices give them away: they know that no animal hunts them for prey. The two Oulhamrs came across them near a glade of turpentine trees. There were four of them hunched over some bones, from which they had chewed all the meat. They didn't run away at the sight of the men, but kept darting watchful glances at them. They yelped softly, ready to take off as soon as they considered the chance comers too close. Nam and Gaw did as Naoh had told them. They placed a quarter of a doe on the ground, and after withdrawing they remained as motionless as the trunks of the turpentine trees. The jackals prowled with short paces on the grass. Their fear lessened at the smell of meat. Although they had often encountered these upright animals, they had never experienced men's tricks; still, judging them stronger than themselves, they followed only at a distance and acted with caution. Hence they prowled for a long time close by the Oulhamrs, circling about, hiding in the glade, and coming out again to circle the motionless bodies. The crescent moon gleamed in the east before their mistrust and their patience had come to an end. Still their approaches were more daring; they came up to twenty paces from the bait and stopped for a long time, murmuring among themselves. Finally their greed decided them. They rushed in a body so as not to give the advantage to any one of them. It was as quick as Naoh had said, but the spears were even quicker. They pierced the flanks of two jackals while the others carried off the prey; then the axes put an end to what life was left in the wounded beasts.

When Nam and Gaw brought back the skins, Naoh exclaimed, "Now we can trick the Kzams, for the odor of the jackals is much more powerful than our own."

Fed with branches and boughs, the fire had revived. Its devouring flames rose smokily over the plain; the sleeping figures could be made out more distinctly with their weapons and provisions; two new watchers had replaced the others, both seated, suspecting no danger.

"Those ones are easier to surprise," said Naoh after considering them attentively. "Nam and Gaw have chased the jackals; the son of the Leopard will hunt in his turn."

He walked down the hill, carrying the skin of a jackal, and disappeared into the underbrush. First he moved at some distance from the Kzams in order not to be discovered. He crossed the undergrowth, climbed among the high grasses, circled a pond shaded by reeds and rushes, crisscrossed among linden trees, and at length turned up about four hundred feet from the fire behind a bush. The watchers hadn't moved. One of them had barely perceived the jackal's smell, which was not a cause of alarm. And Naoh took in all the details of their camp. First he measured the number of warriors and their height. Almost all of them were powerfully built, with deep chests, long arms, and short legs. The Oulhamr felt that none of them could outrun him. Then he examined the lay of the land. An empty space where the earth was bare separated him on the right from a little knoll. Behind it there were some bushes, then a bank of high grass veering to the left. This grass spread out in a sort of promontory up to five or six paces from the fire. Naoh did not hesitate for long. While the watchers' backs were turned he climbed the knoll. He could not go fast. At each movement of the watchers he stopped, flattening himself like a reptile. He felt upon him the double glow of the fire and of the moon like subtle hands. At last he got to the shelter and, slipping beneath the bushes, crossed the grassy strip and reached the fire. He was almost encircled by the sleeping warriors, most of whom were a spear-length away. If the watchmen gave the alarm at the slightest false move, he would be caught. However, he had one chance: the wind was blowing in his direction, carrying the smoke with it and drowning in it his scent and the smell of the jackal. Further, the watchers seemed almost unconscious; they barely raised their heads at intervals.

Naoh appeared in the full moonlight, bounded like a leopard, stretched out his hand, and snatched a brand. Hardly had he gotten back to the strip of grass when a yell went up, while one of the watchers rushed after him and the other hurled a spear. Almost simultaneously, ten silhouettes jumped up. Before any Kzam had found his trail, Naoh had crossed the line at which his retreat could be cut off. With a war cry he dashed straight toward the hillock where Nam and Gaw were waiting for him. The Kzams followed him in a scattered body, grunting like boars. Despite their short legs they were agile, but not quick enough to catch up to the Oulhamr, who bounded before them like a stag as he brandished the torch. He reached the hillock with

an advance of five hundred feet and finding Nam and Gaw on their feet, he cried, "Run ahead!"

Their svelte silhouettes scampered off almost as quickly as their leader. The son of the Leopard followed them effortlessly, stopping now and then to examine the firebrand. He was torn between worrying about the pursuers and his anxiety not to lose the sparkling prey for which he had endured so much suffering. The flame had gone out; there only remained a red glow, lively enough to give Naoh hope that at the first opportunity he could revive it and feed it.

When the moon had gone a third of its course, the Oulhamrs found themselves at a network of ponds. They recognized a track they had already covered, narrow and winding, but solid underfoot, as the base was porphyry. They set off at once, and then made a halt. Two men could hardly advance together, especially for combat; here, it would be easy for the Oulhamrs to outdistance the Kzams. Naoh calculated his chances with the double instinct of animal and man and concluded that he had time to make the fire grow. The red ember had got even smaller; it grew darker and dimmer. The three men looked for grass and dry wood. There were dead reeds, rotting ferns, and sapless willow branches in abundance: all of this vegetation was damp. They tried some branches with slender ends, leaves, and twigs that were short or delicate. The fading ember was barely revived by Naoh's breath. Several times blades of grass were livened with a light glow

(81)

which grew for an instant, stopped wavering on the end of a blade, diminished, and died, killed by the dampness from the water. Then Naoh thought of the jackal hide. He pulled out several tufts of fur and tried to make the flame catch. Some glowed a bit; joy and fear came by turns to the Oulhamrs; but each time, despite infinite precautions, the tiny palpitations stopped and went out. There was no more hope! The ash gave off only a frail glimmer; one last scarlet dot decreased at first to the size of a wasp, then to that of a fly, then to that of a minuscule insect flitting across the surface of the ponds. At last, it was extinguished, and an immense sorrow froze the spirits of the Oulhamrs and left them emptied.

CHAPTER THREE

On the Banks of the Great River

THE chase had lasted two days. It was breathless and full of feints. The Kzams were relentless either out of concern for their future — the three Oulhamrs could be the advance guard of many—or because of their destructive instinct and hatred of strangers. The endurance of the fugitives was equal to their speed. They could have greatly outdistanced their pursuers, but Naoh was set on conquering Fire. At night, after assuring the necessary advance for Nam and Gaw, he prowled about the enemy camp. He slept little but deeply. As the ins and outs of this pursuit required numerous detours, the son of the Leopard was obliged to cut considerably toward the east so that at the end of the second day they came in sight of the Great River. It was at the top of a conical hill from which descended a crevice of porphyry where floods, rain, and vegetation had hewed out banks, dug holes, torn out blocks, but which for hundreds of millennia would resist the brutal and patient ravages of the elements.

Like Fire, the river's waters seemed to the Oulhamrs a being without limits. Like Fire, water diminished, augmented, surged from an invisible source, lashed out across the earth, devouring beasts and men. So Naoh reflected before the inexhaustible floods. But it was necessary to seek shelter. Islands offered refuge against the onslaught of beasts, but were hardly efficacious against men since they would hinder their movements, making the conquest of Fire impossible and exposing them to traps. Naoh preferred the riverbank. He set up camp on a schist boulder which was slightly elevated over the site. The sides were sheer and the top part formed a plateau on which ten men could lie down. They finished the preparations for their camp at twilight. There was enough distance between the Oulhamrs and their pursuers for them to have no fear throughout the night. The air was cold; a few clouds floated in the scarlet sunset. While eating their meal of raw flesh, nuts, and mushrooms, the warriors observed the darkening earth.

In the light, they could still make out the islands if not the far bank of the river. Wild asses passed by, then a herd of horses went down to the river's edge. They were stocky animals whose heads seemed thick because of their matted manes. Their pace was interrupted and sped up nervously; they stood bent over the water, trembling and full of mistrust. Then they drank quickly and raced off. As the night unfolded, jackals yelped and their light silhouettes could be seen sneaking about.

The Oulhamrs slept alternately till the dawn. Then they resumed the descent of the Great River. They were stopped by mammoths. The herd covered an area a thousand feet wide and three times that in length. They pastured, picking tender plants and ripping up roots. Sometimes, rejoicing in their strength, they chased each other over the soft earth or struck each other lightly with their hairy trunks.

Naoh was not in the least afraid of them: he knew that they did not attack any animal unless they were bothered. "Aoum, son of the Crow, made an alliance with the mammoths," he said.

"Why shouldn't we do the same as Aoum?" asked Gaw.

"Aoum understood the mammoths," Naoh objected, "but we do not."

Nevertheless, he was struck by the idea. He thought about it as he circled the gigantic herd at a distance. And translating his thoughts into words, he continued aloud: "The mammoths don't have words like men, to

(85)

talk with each other. They know the call of their leaders; Goun says that they take on command the position assigned to them, and that they take counsel before setting out for new territory. If we were to figure out their signs we could make an alliance with them."

Then he noticed an enormous mammoth who was watching them pass. He stood apart from the herd, farther along the riverbank among some young poplars, grazing on tender shoots. Naoh had never encountered a mammoth of such proportions. His height was fully thirty feet. A thick mane like a lion's grew on his neck; his hairy trunk seemed like an animal in itself, resembling a tree or a snake. The sight of the three men seemed to interest him.

Naoh called, "The mammoths are strong! The Great Mammoth is stronger than all the others. He can crush tiger and lion like worms. He can upset ten aurochs with the shock of his chest. Naoh, Nam, and Gaw are the Great Mammoth's friends!" The mammoth raised his huge ears. He listened to the sounds, then slowly shook his trunk and trumpeted. "The mammoth has understood!" cried Naoh, joyfully. "He knows that the Oulhamrs have acknowledged his power."

Again he cried, "If the sons of the Leopard, the Saiga, and the Poplar recover Fire, they will cook chestnuts as a gift for the Great Mammoth!"

As he spoke, he noticed a pond in which water lilies were growing. Naoh was aware that mammoths liked their stalks, which grow under water. He signaled to his companions and they began to pull up the long brownish plants. When they had made a big pile, they washed them carefully and carried them toward the colossal beast. Fifty paces from him, Naoh resumed speaking:

"Here you are! We have picked these plants for you to graze on. Thus you will know that the Oulhamrs are the friends of the mammoths." And he withdrew.

Curious, the giant approached the stalks. He knew them well; they were to his taste. As he ate them, without haste and with long pauses, he observed the three men. Sometimes he raised his trunk to sniff, then he swung it in a peaceful manner. Then Naoh drew close with unnoticeable movements. He found himself before those colossal feet, under that powerful trunk and the tusks as long as the body of an aurochs. He was like a field mouse facing a panther. In a single move the beast could reduce him to crumbs. The trunk grazed him. It encircled his body and sniffed him. Breathless, Naoh touched the hairy trunk in turn. Then he plucked grass and young shoots which he offered as a sign of alliance.

When they saw Naoh stroking the beast with his hand, Nam and Gaw were filled with joy and pride. "Naoh is making an alliance with the mammoth!" whispered Nam. "Naoh is the most powerful of men."

Meanwhile, the son of the Leopard cried, "Let Nam and Gaw approach in turn in the same manner as Naoh has done. They will pick grass and shoots and offer them to the mammoth." The young warriors listened to him warmly and full of trust. They advanced at the same slow pace as their leader, picking tender grass and young stalks as they went. When they were close, they held out what they had gathered. As Naoh did the same, the mammoth came to eat it. Thus was knitted the alliance of the Oulhamrs with the mammoth.

—•—◄◦⬢◦►—•—

CHAPTER FOUR

The Alliance Between Man and Mammoth

THE moon had grown bigger. It was approaching the night when it would rise as vast as the sun. The Kzams and the Oulhamrs were encamped four miles away from each other along the river. The Kzams occupied a dry strip of territory. They warmed themselves at the roaring fire and ate large pieces of meat, for their hunt had been abundant, while the Oulhamrs were sharing a few roots and the flesh of a wood pigeon in silence amid the cold and humid shadows.

Two miles from the shore the mammoths were asleep

in a glade of sycamores. During the day they had permitted the presence of the three Oulhamrs among them, but with the approach of dusk their humor changed. Either they were fearful of a trap, or else their sleep was hindered by the men's presence. Sensing this, the Oulhamrs had camped beyond the limit at which their scent could be troublesome.

That night Naoh asked his companions, "Are Nam and Gaw ready for exhaustion? Are their limbs supple enough and is their wind strong?" The son of the Poplar replied, "Nam slept part of the day. Why shouldn't he be ready for combat?" And Gaw in turn said, "The son of the Saiga can cross the distance between us and the Kzams at top speed."

"Good! Naoh and his young companions will set out toward the Kzams. They will struggle all night to conquer Fire."

Nam and Gaw rose in one movement and followed their leader. As they approached the camp of the Kzams their speed slowed. Then, at the bend of a willow thicket, still far off, flames shone splendidly, made pale by the moonlight. The Kzams were sleeping. Three watchers tended the fire and kept guard over the night.

Concealed in the vegetation, the prowlers spied on the camp. They held in readiness dry twigs and finely cut branches: the Fire would never again die between their hands before they had imprisoned it in the bark cage lined with flat stones. But how to approach the flame? How to draw away the attention of the Kzams, who were on the lookout since the night that the son of the Leopard had appeared at their fireside?

Naoh said, "Here is the plan. While Naoh goes back up the river, Nam and Gaw will stray into the plain around the camp of the Kzams. At one moment they will hide themselves and at another come into the open. When the enemies rush after them they will take flight, but not at top speed, for the Kzams must have some hope of catching them so that they will pursue for a long time. Nam and Gaw must use all their courage not to flee too quickly. They will draw off the Kzams up to the red rock. If Naoh is not there, they must pass on between the mammoths and the Great River. Naoh will find their trail."

The young men obediently slipped through the underbrush while the son of the Leopard headed for the riverbank. Some time passed. Then Nam showed himself beneath a catalpa tree and disappeared. Then the shadow of Gaw was seen furtively against the grass. The watchers gave the alarm. The Kzams raced up in disorder with long yells and assembled about their leader. He was a warrior of middle height as thickset as a cave bear. Twice he raised his club, barked out commands, and gave the signal. The Kzams spread out in six groups in a semicircle.

Naoh anxiously watched them disappear; then he thought of nothing but conquering the Fire. Four men were guarding it, chosen among the strongest. One especially inspired fear. As thickset as the leader but taller, the very size of his club implied his strength. He was standing full in the light. Naoh could make out his enormous jaw, eyes shadowed by thick eyebrows, short legs of a massive triangular shape. Less heavy, the other three had torsos that were just as thick and long arms with tough muscles. Naoh's position was favorable; a light but continuous wind was blowing toward him, carrying his scent away from the watchers. Jackals were prowling on the savanna, giving off a sharp smell. He had, as well, kept one of the skins. He sneaked up within sixty feet of the fire, and paused for a long time. Then, as the moon came out from behind some poplars, he rose and let out a war cry. Surprised by his sudden appearance, the Kzams stared at him. Their amazement did not last long and they raised their stone axes, clubs, and spears.

Naoh cried, "The son of the Leopard has come across the savannas, forests, mountains, and rivers because his tribe is without Fire. If the Kzams let him take a few brands, he will withdraw without combat."

They did not understand these words from a foreign tongue any more than they would have understood the howl of wolves. Seeing that he was alone, they thought only of killing him, and rushed on him in a body. When the biggest was within range, he threw a flint-tipped spear. He hurled it with strength and skill. The weapon grazed Naoh's shoulder and fell to the damp earth. The Oulhamr, who preferred to conserve his own weapons, picked it up and hurled it back. Whistling through the air, the spear described a curve; it pierced the throat of a Kzam, who staggered and fell.

(92)

His companions riposted simultaneously, letting out doglike cries.

Naoh had only time to dive to the ground to avoid the trenchant points, and the Kzams, believing him hit, rushed up to finish him off. Already he had bounded up and returned the assault. A Kzam, hit in the stomach, stopped pursuing, while the other two hurled their spears one after the other. Blood gushed from Naoh's thigh, but feeling that the wound was superficial, he began to circle about his adversaries, for he was most afraid of being surrounded. He dashed off and came back and at length found himself between the fire and his enemies.

"Naoh is quicker than the Kzams!" he cried. "He will take the Fire and the Kzams will have lost two warriors."

He bounded forward again and came near the flame. But as he stretched out his hands to seize some brands, he noticed with anxiety that they were almost all burned up. He went around the bonfire in the hope of finding a branch that could be carried, but his search was vain. And the Kzams were almost upon him! He wanted to run, but he bumped against a stump and stumbled, so that the enemy managed to bar the way and drive him to the fire.

Although the bonfire filled a considerable space, and was on raised ground, he could have leaped over it and fled. But a great despair filled him at the idea of returning vanquished in the night. Raising his axe and his club together, he accepted combat.

CHAPTER FIVE

The Flight

THE two Kzams had slowed down but were still advancing. The strongest brandished a last javelin, which he hurled almost point-blank. Naoh deflected it with the back of his axe and the delicate weapon was lost among the flames. At the same moment the three clubs hurtled through the air; Naoh's met the other two simultaneously and the crash stopped his adversaries' advance. The weakest of the Kzams had staggered; Naoh saw it, hurled himself upon him, and with an enormous blow broke his neck. He was hit himself:

the knot of a club tore his left shoulder roughly. He barely avoided a blow directly on the head. Breathlessly, he dashed backward to resume his position and wait with his weapon aimed.

Although only one adversary remained, this was the terrible moment. For he hardly had the use of his left hand, while the Kzam stood erect in full force and doubly armed. He was a tall warrior with a wide chest circled by ribs more like an aurochs' than a man's, with arms that exceeded Naoh's in length by a third again. His bowed legs, too short for running, assured him a powerful balance.

Before the decisive attack, he examined the tall Oulhamr slyly. Judging that his advantage would be the more sure if he struck with both hands, he kept only his club; then he took the offensive. The weapons crashed together, almost equal in weight, hewn out of thick oak. The Kzam's blow was stronger than that of Naoh, who could not use his left hand, but the son of the Leopard had parried with a transversal movement. When the Kzam renewed the attack he encountered a void: Naoh had dodged. Now it was he who took the offensive. On the third attempt his club came down like a boulder; it would have crushed his adversary's head, which he saved only by bringing up his sinewy arms. Once more the knotty clubs banged together, and the Kzam withdrew. He responded with a frantic blow which almost tore the club from Naoh; before he could resume his position the hands of the man-eater were raised and came down on him. The Oulhamr could cushion the shock but he could not stop the blow; hit on the head, his knees buckling, he saw the earth, the trees, and the fire revolving around him. In this fatal second his instinct did not abandon him, and a supreme energy rose from the depth of his being as, from an angle, he hurled his club before the adversary had collected himself. Bones cracked; the Kzam crumpled, and his cry was stifled by death.

Then Naoh's joy boiled up like a torrent. With a rasping laugh he looked at the bonfire where flames leaped. Beneath the distant stars, amid the roar of the river, he could hardly conceive of his triumph.

"Naoh is master of Fire!"

His seemed to him the sovereign life in all the world. He slowly circled the red being, stretched out his hand toward it, exposed his chest to that caress that he had missed so long. Then he murmured again, in delight and ecstasy, "Naoh is master of Fire."

At length his happiness abated. He began to fear the return of the Kzams. He had to carry off his conquest. Untying the narrow stones he had carried with him since his departure from the great swamp, he set about joining them with blades of grass, bark, and reeds. As he foraged about the camp a new source of joy came to him: in a hollow in the earth he came upon the cage in which the man-eaters maintained their fire. It was a sort of nest of bark reinforced with flat stones put together with crude skill and patient, solid work. A little flame scintillated in it still. Although Naoh knew how to fabricate fire cages as well as any man of his people, it would have been difficult for him to make one as perfect as this. He would need leisure, a careful choice of stones, and time for the numerous alterations. The Kzams' cage was composed of a triple layer of schist held together on the outside by oak bark. It was tied with flexible little branches, and a cleft allowed it to be carried easily. These cages required constant vigilance. It was necessary to protect the flame against rain and winds, to take care that it did not grow too small or enlarge beyond certain limits fixed by millennial experience, and to renew the bark often.

Naoh was familiar with all the rites transmitted by his ancestors; he lightly revived the fire and dampened the exterior with a little water from a puddle, checked the cleft and the state of the schist. Before escaping, he collected the scattered axes and spears and threw a last glance over the camp and the plain. Two of his adversaries were lying face up, staring at the stars; the other two, in spite of their pain, remained motionless, making believe that they were dead. Prudence and the law of men required that they be finished off. Naoh approached the one who was wounded in the thigh; as he was about to hurl his spear a strange disgust struck him; all hatred had evaporated in his joy and he could not bring himself to do away with another living being. Furthermore, it was more urgent to douse the fire. He scattered the brands with the help of a club left by the vanquished and broke them up into fragments too small to last till the warriors returned; then, tying the wounded with some reeds and branches, he cried:

(97)

"The Kzams did not want to give a brand to the son of the Leopard. Now the Kzams no longer have Fire. They will wander through the night in the cold until they rejoin their people. Thus the Oulhamrs have become stronger than the Kzams!"

Naoh found himself alone at the base of the hill where Nam and Gaw were to rejoin him. He was not surprised: the young warriors must have made wide detours before their pursuers. Having covered his wounds with willow leaves, he sat down near the small fire in which his destiny sparkled. Time flowed on along with the waters of the Great River and the rays of the rising moon. As the moon reached its zenith, Naoh raised his head. In the myriad separate noises he recognized a particular rhythm which belonged to man. It was a rapid footstep, less complicated than the four-legged beasts'. Almost imperceptible at first, it became more precise, and then a breath of wind carried a sudden particular scent his way and the Oulhamr said to himself:

"That is the son of the Poplar who has thrown the enemies off the track."

For there was no indication of pursuit on the plain. Shortly an agile silhouette was cast between two sycamores. Naoh saw that he had not been mistaken; it was Nam who advanced in the silvery film of the moonlight. He hastened to the foot of the hill and the leader asked, "Have the Kzams lost Nam's trail?"

"Nam drew them far to the north, then outstripped them and for a long time walked in the river. Then he stopped, and he no longer saw, heard, or smelled the Kzams."

"Good," said Naoh, laying his hand on the youth's shoulder. "Nam has been agile and skillfull. But what has become of Gaw?"

"The son of the Saiga has been followed by another band of Kzams. Nam did not cross his trail."

"We will wait for Gaw! And now look, Nam."

Naoh led his companion behind the hill where, in a notch, Nam saw a little flame gleaming warmly. "There!" said the leader. "Naoh has conquered Fire."

The young man let out a great cry. His eyes grew big with the light; he knelt before the son of the Leopard and murmured, "Naoh is as skilled as a whole band of men. He will be the great chief of the Oulhamrs and no enemy will be able to resist him."

They sat down by the little fire, and it was as if the bonfire of nights protected them with its angry strength at the entrance to their native caves under the cold stars, among the fireflies of the Great Swamp. The idea of the long return was no longer painful to them; when they left the land of the Great River, the Kzams would not pursue them. They would cross regions where only beasts prowled in the solitude. They dreamed on a long time. The future was upon them, and for them it was full of promise. But when the moon began to grow in the western sky, fear lay in their hearts.

"What is keeping Gaw?" whispered Naoh. "Has he been unable to throw off the Kzams? Has he been stopped by a swamp or caught in a trap?"

The plain was mute. The animals were silent. The wind grew calm over the river and spread out in the aspen trees; only the muted noise of the waters could be heard. Must they wait till the dawn or begin the search for the missing one? It was strangely disagreeable to Naoh to leave Nam to guard the Fire. On the other hand, the image of the young warrior pursued by the Kzams bothered him. For the sake of the Fire, he could abandon him to his fate, and it even was his duty to do so, but he had developed a certain tenderness toward his companions.

"Naoh will look for Gaw's trail!" he said finally. "He will leave the son of the Poplar to guard the Fire. Nam will have no rest. He must dampen the bark when it is too hot. He must never wander off for long except to go to the river and back."

"Nam will guard the Fire as if it were his own life," the young Oulhamr stoutly replied. He added with pride, "Nam knows how to maintain the flame. His mother taught him when he was as little as a wolf cub."

"That's good. If Naoh has not returned when the sun reaches the top of the poplars, Nam must take refuge near the mammoths, and if Naoh has not returned before the end of the day, Nam must flee alone toward the hunting grounds of the Oulhamrs."

He went off. His whole being vibrated with distress, and many times he looked back toward the diminishing silhouette of Nam, toward the little cage of fire in which he imagined he could still see a weak glimmer, although it had already mingled with the moonlight.

CHAPTER SIX

The Search for Gaw

To find Gaw's track he first had to return toward the camp of the Kzams. He walked more slowly; his shoulder burned him under the willow leaves which he had pressed on it and his head was humming. He felt a pain in the spot where he had been hit by the club, and he was disconsolate to note that after he had conquered Fire his task still remained as harsh and uncertain. He arrived in this state at the same ash grove where he had sighted the camp of the Kzams with his young companions. Then a red bonfire had outshone the rising moon: now the camp was mournful, the burning logs dispersed by Naoh were all extinguished, and the silvery light of night lay on the immobile expanse: all that was heard was the intermittent moan of a wounded man. Having consulted each of his senses, Naoh was persuaded that the pursuers had not returned. He walked toward the camp. The moans of the wounded man stopped; it seemed as if there were only corpses left. He did not tarry but walked in the direction in which Gaw had fled, and he recovered his trail. At first it was easy to follow, for it had been trodden by numerous Kzams almost in a straight line; then it veered and wound between some hillocks, twisted back on itself, and crossed through some underbrush. A pond cut across it abruptly: Naoh picked it up again only at the bend in the riverbank, damp now, as if Gaw and the others had dived into the water.

Before a sycamore wood, the Kzams must have divided into several bands; all the same, Naoh managed to distinguish the right direction and walked on for another mile or so. But then he had to stop. Thick clouds engulfed the moon and the dawn had not yet revealed itself.

Standing, Naoh ate a piece of dried flesh; then he bent over the ground and resumed the trail. It led him a few thousand feet on; leaving the wood, it crossed a sandy plain where the grass was sparse and shrubby trees were stunted; it wound through a terrain where red reeds were rotting at the edge of ponds; it climbed a hill and wound through knolls; finally it stopped at the edge of the river which Gaw must certainly have crossed. Naoh crossed it in turn and after surveying the region extensively, he discovered that two trails converged: Gaw might have been sighted by the Kzams.

At this, the leader reflected that it might be right to abandon the fugitive to his fate in order not to risk for the sake of a single existence his own life and Nam's and the Fire. But the pursuit had exasperated him; a sort of fever throbbed at his temples, and an obstinate hope prevailed in spite of all; he was also simply caught up in the momentum of the thing begun.

Besides the two parties of Kzams, whose trick Naoh had just recognized, he had to take into consideration the group which had pursued Nam and which, after so many twists and turns, had had the time to assume an advantageous position: that is, if it had not also divided into the surrounding groups. Confident of his superior speed and his shrewdness, the son of the Leopard did not hesitate to follow Gaw's track, hardly even stopping to examine the area. The ground became hard: granite appeared beneath a poor topsoil of a bluish hue. Then an escarpment appeared which Naoh decided to climb because the tracks were now quite recent, so that from the top he could hope to have a view of Gaw's silhouette or of a band of pursuers. The Oulhamr slipped into the underbrush and made it to the top of the hill.

He let out a soft exclamation. Gaw had just appeared on a strip of red earth, an earth which seemed to have been watered by the blood of numberless herds. A thousand feet behind him the men with thick torsos and short legs advanced, spaced at regular distances from each other; to the north, a second group poured out of the forest. Despite the length of the pursuit, the son of the Saiga did not seem to be exhausted. The Kzams showed at least as much fatigue as he did. During the long autumn night, Gaw had not broken into a run, except to evade ambushes or to worry the enemy; unfortunately the maneuvers of the Kzams had made him lose his way. He pushed on aimlessly, having lost the sense of whether he was at the foot of the rock where he was supposed to join his leader or midway up its slope.

Naoh could follow all the ins and outs of the chase. Gaw was running toward a pine wood to the northeast. The first group followed him, forming a broken line which cut his retreat along a distance of a thousand feet. The second group, which came from the north, was beginning to curve in order to get to the wood at the same time as the fugitive; but while he was approaching it from the southwest, they must get there from the direction of the sunrise. This situation was not desperate, nor even very unfavorable, provided the fugitive veered toward the northwest as soon as he found himself in cover. His speed would enable him to get a suitable advance, and if Naoh joined him at that point they could head in the direction of the Great River.

At a glance Naoh perceived the favorable route. It was an expanse of undergrowth where he would be hidden, which would take him to the level of the wood in the direction of the sunset. He was just getting ready

to go down the hill when he noticed a new circum-
stance, much more ominous, which made him start: a
third group was appearing, this time in the northwest.
Gaw could not avoid being trapped except by fleeing
to the west at great speed. He did not seem to be aware
of his peril, as he was taking a straight course. Once
more, Naoh hesitated between the necessity of safe-
guarding the Fire, Nam, and himself and the tempta-
tion to come to Gaw's assistance: once more he yielded
to the enormous force which drives man and beast to
pursue the task begun.

After a long look at the area whose every detail was
fixed in his mind, the son of the Leopard went down
the hill. He followed the underbrush to its eastern limit,
then he cut across some high blue and reddish grass;
and as his speed far exceeded that of Gaw and the
Kzams, who were winded, he came in sight of the
wood before the fugitive had entered it. Now he had
to make his presence known. He imitated the belling of
an elk, which he repeated three times: it was a signal
familiar to the Oulhamrs. But the distance was too
great; Gaw might perhaps have heard it under ordi-
nary conditions, but exhausted and with his attention
upon the pursuers, the call escaped him. So Naoh decided to become visible; he dashed out of the high
grass, rushed in front of the enemy, and let out his
war cry. A long yell, repeated by the parties of the
Kzams which were coming from the west and from
the east of the wood, reverberated through space. Gaw
stopped, his knees trembling, full of joy and astonish-

ment; then, putting on all his speed, he rushed toward
the son of the Leopard. Already the latter, sure of being followed, was taking the line open to him in flight.
But the third party of Kzams were alerted and had
also changed their route so that they rushed up to cut
off the retreat, while the first pursuers dashed at great
speed in a direction almost parallel to the fugitive.
These maneuvers succeeded: the way to the west was
blocked at once by the Kzams and by a mass of rocks
that was almost inaccessible, and it was becoming
impossible to veer to the southwest where some of the
warriors were forming a semicircle. As Naoh led Gaw
straight toward the rocks, the Kzams, tightening their
circle, let out a cry of triumph. Several got within fifty
feet of the Oulhamrs and hurled their spears, but Naoh
plunged through a curtain of underbrush, leading his
companion through a passage he had seen from the top
of the hill. The Kzams yelled; several of them in turn
scrambled through the defile and the others circled the
obstacle.

However, Naoh and Gaw were fleeing at top speed,
and would have gotten a considerable advance if the
terrain had not been so rough, uneven, and varying.
When they came out the other side of the mass of
rocks, three Kzams turned up from the north and cut
their retreat. Naoh could have veered up the slope, but
he heard the growing sound of the pursuit. He knew that
on this side also his way would be blocked. All hesitation would now be fatal. With his club in one hand
and his axe in the other, he made a dash right at the

attackers, while Gaw's fist tightened on the spear. Fearing that the Oulhamrs would escape, the three Kzams had split up. Naoh rushed at the one on his left; he was a very young warrior, light and flexible, who raised his axe to parry the attack. A blow of the club disposed of his weapon and a second one downed him. The two other Kzams had rushed upon Gaw, counting on doing away with him quickly enough to reunite their forces against Naoh. The young Oulhamr had throw a javelin and wounded one of the aggressors slightly. Before he could strike with his spear, he was hit in the chest. He put himself on guard by a rapid withdrawal and a leap to the side. While one of the Kzams was attacking him from the front at great speed, the other was trying to strike him from behind: Gaw would have succumbed had not Naoh arrived. His enormous club came down with the noise of a falling tree. One Kzam sank to the ground; the other beat a retreat toward a group of warriors who were advancing at top speed from the north. It was too late. The Oulhamrs escaped encirclement and fled to the west along a line that was not barred by the enemy, and at each stride they augmented their lead.

They ran a long time over the resounding earth, through the mire and among whistling grasses, through the brush, over peat bogs, sometimes climbing slopes and sometimes rushing headlong down them. Long before the sun was in the middle of the sky, they had gained an advance of a mile. Often they hoped that the enemy would stop pursuing, but when they reached

a peak they always discovered behind them the relentless pack of Kzams.

Meanwhile, Gaw was weakening. His wound had
not stopped bleeding. Sometimes it was only a tiny
trickle: despite the furious dash, the wound seemed
closed; but after the more demanding efforts or after
several wrong moves in a morass, the blood began to
spurt. When they came to some young poplars, Naoh
made a pad out of leaves, but the wound continued to
bleed under the bandage. Little by little, Gaw's speed
became equal to, and then less than, the Kzams'. Now
each time the fugitives looked back, the advance guard
of the Kzams had gained ground, and with a deep rage
the son of the Leopard realized that if Gaw did not
pick up strength they would be caught before they
could rejoin the herd of mammoths. But Gaw did not
gain strength. There came a hill which he climbed with
extreme difficulty; at the top, his legs trembled, his face
became the color of ashes, his heart almost gave out, and
he staggered. And Naoh, turning toward the wild
bunch who were beginning to climb the slope, saw
how much their speed had lessened.

"If Gaw can run no more," he said in a hollow voice,
"the Kzams will catch us before we get in sight of the
River."

"Gaw's sight is dark, his ears whirr like crickets,"
stammered the young warrior. "Let the son of the Leopard go on alone. Gaw will die for Fire and for Naoh."

"Gaw will not die yet!"

And turning toward the Kzams, Naoh let out a

furious war cry. Then, throwing Gaw on his shoulders, he resumed the flight. First, his great courage and impressive musculature permitted him to keep his advance. He bounded over the sloping ground, carried forward by the weight. As flexible as the branches of an ash, his knees sustained this continual decline. At the foot of the hill, his breathing quickened and his feet grew heavier. Without his wound, which burned dully, and without the blow on his head which made his ears hum, even with Gaw on his shoulder he could have outstripped the Kzams with their stocky legs, exhausted by the long race. No beast of the steppe could have sustained so long and arduous a trial. Now, without relief, the distance separating him from the Kzams grew smaller. He could hear their feet scrape the earth and rebound. He knew at each moment how much they were gaining. They were at five hundred paces, then at four hundred, then at two hundred. Then the son of the Leopard put Gaw down on the ground, and with haggard eyes he experienced the supreme hesitation.

"Gaw, son of the Saiga," he said at last, "Naoh cannot carry you any longer before the Kzams!"

Having rested on his leader's shoulder in spite of the jouncing, Gaw raised himself and stretched his arms, and the Kzams, who were within sixty feet, raised their spears to begin the fight. Naoh turned to face them, having resolved not to flee till the last moment. The first projectiles whizzed; hurled from too far, most of them fell without reaching the Oulhamrs. A single one grazed Gaw's leg, cutting him as lightly as a wild-

rose thorn. In answer, Naoh hit the closest enemy.
Next he pierced the chest of a warrior who was running with great strides. This double exploit threw the
advance guard of the aggressors into a panic. They let
out a terrible yell, and stopped to await reinforcements. The pause was favorable to the Oulhamrs. The
cut seemed to have awakened Gaw; with a hand that
was still weak, he seized a spear and brandished it,
waiting for the enemy to come within range.

Seeing this gesture, Naoh asked, "Has Gaw recovered his strength? He must flee! Naoh will hold the
pursuers at bay."

The young warrior hesitated, but Naoh added,
briefly, "Run!"

Gaw started to flee, at first with a stiff stride, then
growing surer as he went. Naoh, slow and menacing,
withdrew holding a spear in each hand, and the Kzams
hesitated. Finally, their leader ordered the attack. Spears
whistled and the men leaped. Naoh stopped two more
warriors in their tracks and took off.

The chase resumed across the endless land. Gaw's
legs at times were strong and at times they buckled, his
muscles softened, and his breathing was harsh. Naoh
dragged him by the hand. The Kzams had not lost
their advantage; they followed at a sustained jog without even hastening, confident of their endurance. Soon
Naoh could no longer drag his companion; fatigue and
fever increased his wound, his head buzzed, and to
make things worse, he hit his foot against a rock. The
chief was somber. He listened to the jogging footsteps

of the enemy; again they were only two hundred feet away, then a hundred as the fugitives climbed a slope. The son of the Leopard gathered his great forces and maintained the distance to the top of the hill and there, looking far to the east, his heart pounded with lassitude and hope at once and he cried:

"The Great River . . . the mammoths!"

The vast water was indeed there, sparkling among the poplars, alders, and ash. The herd was there also, less than a mile away, grazing on roots and young trees. Naoh dashed ahead, dragging Gaw, in a burst which gained them a hundred feet. It was the last gasp. They lost this slight advance again step by step. The Kzams let out their war cry. When Naoh and Gaw were two thousand feet beyond the top of the hillock, the Kzams were almost on them. They maintained their speed, all the more sure of catching the Oulhamrs, since they would corner them in front of the herd of mammoths. They knew that in spite of their peaceful indifference, these animals would not suffer an alien presence, and so would trample the fugitives. All the same, the pursuers didn't fail to shorten the gap. Their breathing could now be heard, and it was still necessary to cross a thousand feet more. Naoh let out a long cry for help, at which a man was seen emerging from a grove of plane trees. Then one of the enormous beasts raised his trunk and gave a strident trumpet. It ran forward, followed by three others, straight toward the son of the Leopard. The Kzams, aghast and delighted, stopped. They had only to wait for the Oulhamrs' retreat to take aim and destroy them. However, Naoh continued to run another hundred paces, and then turning toward the Kzams, his face hollow with fatigue and his eyes gleaming with triumph, he cried:

"The Oulhamrs have made alliance with the mammoths! Naoh laughs at the Kzams."

As he spoke, the mammoths arrived. The Kzams were stupefied to see the biggest of them put his trunk on the Oulhamr's shoulder. And Naoh continued:

"Naoh has captured the Fire. He has struck down four warriors in the camp. He has killed four others during the pursuit!"

The Kzams replied with furious yells, but as the mammoths kept advancing they hastily withdrew, for they had no more conceived that man could combat these colossal herds than had the Oulhamrs.

CHAPTER SEVEN

Life with the Mammoths

NAM had guarded the Fire well. It burned clear and pure in its cage when Naoh returned to it. And although he had been extremely harassed and his wound bit at his flesh like a wolf and his head buzzed with fever, the son of the Leopard experienced a great moment of happiness.

Naoh then picked roots and tender plants in homage to the giant mammoth, for he figured that to be lasting, the alliance must be renewed each day. Only then did he go off to choose a retreat in the center of the great herd to lie down while Nam took the watch.

"If the mammoths leave this pastureland," said Nam, "I will waken the son of the Leopard."

"The pasturage is abundant," replied Naoh. "The mammoths will graze till evening."

He fell into a sleep deep as death. When he awoke the sun was setting across the savanna. Schist-colored clouds had piled up and softly cradled the yellow disk which looked like a vast water lily. Naoh felt his limbs aching at the joints; fever played along his spine and in his head. But the humming in his ears was lessening and the pain in his shoulder abating. He got up and looked at the Fire.

"Have the Kzams returned?" he asked Nam.

"They have not yet gone away. They are waiting at the river's edge in front of an island with high poplars."

"Good!" replied the son of the Leopard. "They will have no fire during the damp nights. They will lose courage and return to their people. Nam can sleep in his turn."

While Nam stretched out on the leaves and lichen, Naoh examined Gaw, whose arms were flailing as he dreamed. The young man was weak; his skin burning hot. He breathed hoarsely, but no blood flowed from his chest. Then Naoh bent over the Fire. He had a great desire to see it blazing amid a bonfire of dry branches, but he put it off for a later day, for he first had to gain the permission of the leader of the mammoths for the Oulhamrs to spend the night in his camp. Naoh found the Great Mammoth standing solitary, ac-

cording to his habit, the better to watch over his herd
and observe the area. He was grazing on shrubby trees
whose heads hardly rose above the ground. The son of
the Leopard pulled up roots of edible ferns and moved
toward him. The beast stopped grazing at his approach;
he softly swayed his hairy trunk and took a few steps
in Naoh's direction. Seeing his hands full of food, he
appeared content. Naoh held out the roots and whispered:

"Leader of the Mammoths, the Kzams have not yet
left the river. The Oulhamrs are stronger than the
Kzams, but there are only three of us while there are
more than two times two hands of them. They will kill
us if we stray from the mammoths."

His hunger satisfied from a day at pasture, the mammoth ate slowly. When he had finished, he looked at
the sunset and then lay down on the ground, while his
trunk half encircled the man's torso. Naoh concluded
that the alliance was complete; that he and Gaw could
wait in the camp of the mammoths till they were healed,
protected from the Kzams, and from the lions, tigers,
and gray bears. Perhaps he would even be allowed to
light the fire and taste the sweetness of cooked roots,
chestnuts, and meat.

Naoh no longer feared the Kzams; his alliance with
the mammoths had become perfect. Each morning he
was surer of his strength. His head no longer buzzed.
The wound in his shoulder, which was not deep, closed
rapidly and all his fever went away. Gaw was healing
also. Often the three Oulhamrs, standing on a hillock,

defied their adversaries. They let out war cries and brandished their spears. But the Kzams prowled in the brush among the reeds, on the savanna, or beneath the maples, sycamores, ash, and poplars. At times a hairy chest was suddenly visible, or a head with long hair, or else silhouettes whose forms were hard to make out slid about in the half-light. And although they were without fear, the Oulhamrs detested this evil presence. It kept them from reconnoitering in the countryside; it menaced their future, for they must soon leave the mammoths to return to the north. The son of the Leopard thought out ways of throwing the enemy off their track. Three times a day he gathered nourishment for the Great Mammoth and spent long periods seated next to him, trying to understand his language and to make him understand his own.

On the third day, the presence of the Kzams became unbearable. Naoh had recovered all his strength, and inactivity weighed on him. Seeing several hairy chests appear among the plane trees, he was filled with rage and exclaimed:

"The Kzams will not feed on the flesh of Naoh, Gaw, and Nam."

Then he called his companions together and said:

"I will make the Great Mammoth follow me. Thus we will be able to combat the Kzams."

When they had hidden the Fire in a safe place, the Oulhamrs set to work. By offering food, they led the Great Mammoth away from the camp. Now and then Naoh spoke to him softly. After a certain distance, the

huge beast hesitated. His sense of responsibility to the herd grew with each stride. He stopped and turned his head to the west. Then he ceased to advance, and when Naoh cried to him the Great Mammoth replied with a cry. The son of the Leopard retraced his steps and put his hand on the trunk of his ally and said:

"The Kzams are hidden in the bushes. If the mammoths would help us to fight them, they would not dare to prowl around the camp."

The Great Mammoth remained impassive. He continued to consider the herd far behind him, for whose safety he was responsible. Naoh knew that the Kzams were hidden several arrow-shots away and could not bring himself to abandon the attack. Followed by Nam and Gaw, he slipped into the vegetation. Javelins whistled through the air. Several Kzams stood up in the underbrush to see the enemy better, and Naoh let out a long, strident call for help. Then the great mammoth appeared to understand. He let out a terrifying trumpet which called up the herd, and bore down on the Kzams. Naoh brandished his club; Nam and Gaw held their axes in their left hands and spears in their right, letting out a warlike clamor. The terrified Kzams dispersed across the brush, but rage had seized the Great Mammoth. He charged the fugitives as he would have a rhinoceros, while at the Great River the herd could be seen rushing in a wild mass.

The Great Mammoth reached the first fugitive. The Kzam threw himself to the ground, howling with terror, but the muscular trunk curled to seize him. It hurled the man vertically ten feet from the ground, and as he fell a huge foot crushed him like an insect.

The herd arrived. It surged over the brush; a tidal wave of muscles engulfed the plain. The earth palpitated. All the Kzams who were in their way from the Great River to the knolls and ash woods were reduced to a bloody pulp. Only then did the fury of the mammoths abate. The Great Mammoth halted at the foot of a hillock, giving the signal to stop. They all stopped with glowing eyes and bodies shaking with energy. The few Kzams who had escaped disaster fled in bewilderment toward the south. Their ambush was to be feared no more; they had renounced forever tracking the Oulhamrs to devour them. They carried to their tribe the astonishing news of the alliance between the mammoths and the men of the north whose legend would be perpetuated across numberless generations.

After the stampede, the mammoths continued to descend the Great River, and soon their route separated from the one the Oulhamrs must take to return to the tribe. For the river, which at first took a northern route, veered to the east and would soon flow back toward the south. Unless the herd would consent to abandon the neighborhood of the riverbanks, Naoh was going to have to leave them. After so much security, the solitude seemed more bitter. One morning, Naoh stopped in front of the Great Mammoth and said to him:

"The son of the Leopard has made alliance with the herd of mammoths. His heart is content with them. He would follow them for seasons without number. But he must again see Gammla at the edge of the great swamp. His route is to the north and to the west."

He let out a long sigh and called his companions. Then, seeing the last of the herd disappear, he climbed a hillock. From afar, he gazed at the Great Mammoth, who had welcomed them and saved them from the Kzams. His heart was heavy with fear and sorrow.

◄◄ Part Three ►►

CHAPTER ONE

The Little Men

HEAVY rains came. Naoh, Nam, and Gaw bogged down in flooded regions, wandered beneath rotting branches, crossed hilltops, and rested in the shelter of foliage and in the hollows of rocks and fissures in the ground. The Fire was their joy and constant concern. Sometimes when the rain was falling too thick and uninterrupted, a shelter became necessary. If the rocks, trees, and soil did not offer one, they had to dig one out or build it. Thus they lost many days; they also lost time circumventing obstacles. But had they tried to take a straighter course, they might have stretched out their journey even more. They were heading for the country of the Oulhamrs, guided by instinct and by the sun.

They came to the edge of a sandy terrain cut by granite and basalt deposits; it seemed to bar the whole northeast, a bleak, miserable, and threatening landscape. Two days passed before they saw the end of the plains and naked dunes. They were hungry, as the alert and swift prey escaped their traps; they were thirsty because the rain had lessened and the sand drank up the water. More than once, they feared the death of the Fire. On the third day, the grass grew less sparse and tough; pines gave place to sycamores, plane trees, and poplars; ponds became more frequent. The sky lowered, full of opaque clouds endlessly opening. The Oulhamrs spent the night under an aspen tree, having lit a pile of spongy wood and leaves, which hissed under the downpour and gave off suffocating smoke. Naoh took the first watch, and then it was Nam's turn. The young Oulhamr walked about the fire, intent on reviving it with a pointed stick and on drying out twigs to feed it.

The warrior suddenly shivered. His senses became alert. He recognized that something living was prowling around the fire, and he gently nudged his leader. Naoh jumped up at once, and in his turn examined the night. He knew that Nam was not mistaken: something alive was moving in the humid vegetation. Its scent was masked by the smoke, and yet the son of the Leopard surmised that men were present. With his spear

(126)

he gave three hard blows to the hottest part of the bonfire; the flames leaped, mingling scarlet and sulphur. At
a distance, silhouettes concealed themselves. Naoh wakened Gaw. "Men have come," he whispered.

Side by side, they tried to overtake the shadows, but
nothing appeared. There was no strange noise to trouble the patter of the rain, no odor gave a clue in the
gusts of wind. Where had the danger gone? Was it a
band or just a few men haunting the solitude? Which
way should they go — to follow them or escape?

"Guard the Fire!" Naoh said at length.

His companions watched his body fade into the distance, diminish like smoke, and become absorbed by
the unknown. After a detour, he headed toward the
bushes where he had seen the men hiding. The fire
guided him. Although he was invisible himself, he
could distinguish something the color of red twilight.
He stopped frequently, his club and axe ready. Thanks
to the damp earth and his own caution, the most alert
wolf would not have heard his footstep. He stopped
before reaching the bushes. Time passed. He heard
nothing but the raindrops, plants rustling, and the flight
of a few animals. Changing direction, he passed by the
bushes and retraced his steps. No track was to be seen.
He was not surprised, having instinctively expected
this, and he went on in the direction of a mound which
he had noted in the twilight. After feeling his way a
bit, he reached the hillock and climbed it. Farther down
in a fold in the hill, a light showed through the mist;
Naoh recognized a man-made fire. It was at some dis-

tance and the air was unclear, so that he could barely make out a few twisted silhouettes. But he had no doubt of what they were: he trembled. This time the danger was greater, for the strangers had recognized the Oulhamrs' presence before they had been discovered themselves.

Naoh returned to his companions, at first very slowly and then faster when their fire became visible.

"Some men are over there!" he whispered. He pointed to the east, sure of his sense of direction. "We must light the Fire in the cage again," he added after a pause.

This job was confided to Nam and Gaw, while he threw branches around the pile of burning logs in order to make a sort of barrier; whoever approached could make out the light from the flames but could not see whether the fire was attended. When the cage was ready and the provisions shared out, Naoh ordered their departure. The rain had become lighter and there was not a breath of wind. If the strangers did not bar the road or discover their flight immediately, they would notice the fire burning alone and, believing it defended, would not attack until they had made a number of feints; thus Naoh could gain a considerable advance.

Toward dawn the rain stopped. A weak light showed in the sky and the dawn came feebly across the cloudbanks. For some time the Oulhamrs climbed a slight incline. When they were higher they saw at first only the savanna, underbrush, and forests the color of clay or ochre with blue and russet islands.

"The men have lost our trail," murmured Nam. But

Naoh responded, "The men are following us!"

In fact, two figures appeared at a fork in the river, swiftly followed by many others. In spite of the distance Naoh judged their stature to be strangely short; the kind of weapons they were carrying could not be made out. They did not see the Oulhamrs hidden among the trees, and they stopped at intervals to verify the tracks. Their number grew until the son of the Leopard estimated it at about twenty. They did not seem to have the same agility as the fugitives.

Unless they retraced their steps, the Oulhamrs had to cross an almost empty zone of short grass. The best thing would be to proceed without detours and to count on the enemy's tiring. As the slope went down again the three men gained a good distance without getting tired, and when they turned around they saw the pursuers gesticulating on the summit, having lost more ground.

When they regained the savanna Naoh was glad, and at that moment there appeared from their left a group of men whose structure he recognized. Were these the same ones they had sighted earlier who, accustomed to the territory, had taken a shorter route than the fugitives? Or was it another band of the same race? They were near enough for a clear view of the smallness of their bodies: the forehead of the tallest one would hardly have reached to Naoh's chest. They had rather square heads with angular features, skin the color of red ochre, and though they seemed frail, their agile movements and bright eyes indicated a race full of life.

At the sight of the Oulhamrs they let out a cry which resembled the croaking of crows, and brandished spears and javelins.

The son of the Leopard stared at them in stupefaction. Except for the hair that grew in little tufts on their cheeks and the aged look of some of them, despite their weapons and the size of their chests, he would have taken them for half-grown children. At first he did not imagine that they would dare to risk combat; they hesitated. And when the Oulhamrs raised their clubs and spears, and Naoh's voice, which dominated theirs as the thundering of a lion dominates the call of crows, resounded over the plain, they slunked off. But they must have been in a warlike humor; their cries were taken up again menacingly. Then they dispersed in a semicircle. Naoh realized that they wanted to get an aim. Fearing their trickery more than their strength, he gave the signal to retreat. The Oulhamrs easily out-distanced their pursuers, who were slower than the Kzams: if no obstacles occurred, they would not be caught. But Naoh was worried about the terrain and possible traps. He ordered Nam and Gaw to continue running, and putting down the fire cage, he began to observe the enemy. In their excitement they had gotten separated. Three or four of the most agile were in advance of the group. The son of the Leopard lost no time. He picked up some stones to add to his weapons and ran at top speed toward the little men. One of them who seemed to be the leader let out a shrill cry; they all stopped. Already Naoh was close to the one he wanted to reach. He shouted, "Naoh, the son of the Leopard, does not wish ill to you men. He will not strike if you stop pursuing!"

They all listened with impassive faces. Seeing that the Oulhamr was not advancing, they resumed their enveloping attack. So Naoh whirled a stone around in his hand and cried, "The son of the Leopard will beat the Little Men!"

Three or four javelins were shot at this menacing gesture: their range was very inferior to what the Oulhamrs could achieve. He threw the stone. It struck the man he had aimed at and made him fall. Quickly he hurled a second stone, which missed, then a third, which struck the chest of a warrior. Then he made a derisive sign, holding up a fourth stone, and hurled a spear with a terrible countenance. The Little Men understood signs better than the Oulhamrs and the Kzams because they made less use of articulate language. They knew that the spear would be more dangerous than the stones; the ones in front moved back to the group, and the son of the Leopard withdrew at a slow pace. They followed him at a distance; each time one of them got ahead of his companions, Naoh let out a roar and brandished his weapons. Thus the Little Men knew that there was more danger in splitting up than in staying together, and Naoh, having accomplished his aim, moved on.

The Oulhamrs fled for the rest of the day, and when they stopped, the Little Men had not been within sight for a long time.

CHAPTER TWO

The Granite Ridge

Toward the middle of the next day bushes and shrubbery became more frequent; they had to constantly keep an eye on the narrowing horizon. All the same, Naoh did not believe that the Little Men were close. If they had not given up pursuit, they must be following the track of the Oulhamrs at a considerable distance.

Their meat supply was finished, so the three men drew closer to the riverbank, where prey abounded. They failed to catch a bustard, which took refuge on an island, but afterwards they captured a small bream at the head of a stream. Then Naoh speared a water rail and Nam caught a few eels. They lit a fire of dry grass and branches, delighted with the smell of meat roasting. Life was good, strength filled their youthful limbs; they believed they had tired out their pursuers.

They were just finishing gnawing the bones of the water rail when some animals leaped from the bushes. Naoh realized that they were fleeing from an enemy. He got up in time to spot a furtive form among the vegetation.

"The Little Men have returned!" he said.

Danger was greater than before, for the Little Men could follow the Oulhamrs under cover, cutting off their route by ambush. A strip of almost bare territory lay ahead between a swamp and the brush. The Oulhamrs hastily fueled the cage and collected their weapons and the meat that was left. Nothing hindered their departure. If the enemy followed them through the brush they would lose ground, hindered by the vegetation and handicapped by their slower speed. The arid heath widened, then grew narrow through some trees, shrubs, and high grass. Yet the ground remained solid, and Naoh was sure of having outdistanced the Little Men: while no obstacle came up they would keep their advantage.

But there were obstacles. The swamp sent out tongues into the plain, deep havens, pools, canals choked with viscous plants. The fugitives saw their route endlessly obstructed: they had to turn, make detours, and even backtrack. At length they were hemmed in on a granite ridge touched on the right by a wide stretch of water and flooded on the left by autumn freshets. The ridge sloped down and disappeared; the Oulhamrs found themselves a target on three sides; they either had to back up or expect chance attacks.

It was a crucial moment. If the Little Men were at the entrance of the granite strip, all retreat would be impossible. The Oulhamrs rapidly tried the exits. In the distance a brownish mass rose which could be either an island or the resumption of the ridge. Gaw and Naoh looked for a ford and found nothing but deep water and the treacherous mire and ooze. So their last chance lay in turning back. They quickly decided on that and set about it in haste. They covered two thousand feet and came out of the swamp again, facing tufty vegetation interrupted by only occasional islands and short grass. Nam, who was in the lead, stopped abruptly and said, "The Little Men are there."

Naoh picked up stones and threw them rapidly at the thicket Nam had pointed to: slight but unmistakable sounds of movement indicated the enemy's whereabouts. Retreat had become impossible. They had to prepare for combat. To avoid being surrounded, they took up a position on the ridge; with the light from the fire they would be shielded from surprise attack.

Naoh, Nam, and Gaw let out their war cry. And as they brandished their weapons, Naoh cried, "The Little Men are wrong to pursue the Oulhamrs, who are as strong as bears and as agile as saigas. If the Little Men attack, they will die! Naoh alone will kill a great number. Nam and Gaw will also kill. Do Little Men want to let so many of their warriors die to destroy three Oulhamrs?"

From everywhere among the bushes and the high grasses, voices came. The son of the Leopard realized that the enemies were ready for war and death.

At first the Little Men did not appear, fearing an ambush or waiting for a wrong move from the Oulhamrs, but they showed themselves at the end of the day and throughout the night. By the light of the fire they could be seen springing from their hiding places, advancing up to the granite ridge and then retreating. Despite the simulated attack, the aggressors stayed out of range.

Toward dawn there was a sudden noise and it seemed as if the bushes were advancing like living beings. When the day broke Naoh saw a pile of branches obstructing the approach to the granite strip: the Little Men let out warlike cries. The Oulhamrs realized that protected by the branches the Little Men would be able to hurl their spears without coming into the open and could jump out in full number for a decisive attack.

By night the situation of the three warriors was becoming more and more serious. Seated by the fire, Naoh was overcome by anxiety. He had fortified the shelter, but he knew that soon his companions would be weaker than the Little Men and he himself would probably hurl the spear with less accuracy, his club strike with less killing force. Instinct told him to flee to the protection of the dark. But they would have to surprise the Little Men and force a passage, which was probably impossible. Fever came over him; he sat up and prodded the fire, after which he walked in the direction of the enemy. He gritted his teeth at the sight of the pile of branches, which had been drawn nearer; soon the enemy would be in a position to begin the attack. Suddenly a sharp cry pierced the air, and a vague form emerged from the water which Naoh recognized as a man. He was limping and blood flowed from his thighs; his shape was strange, almost without shoulders and with a very narrow head. At first it seemed that the Little Men had not seen him; then a clamor arose and javelins and stakes whistled through the air. The figure evoked conflicting reactions from Naoh, but then his fury arose against the attackers, and he ran toward the wounded man as he would have run to save Nam or Gaw. A spear struck him on the shoulder without stopping him. He let out a war cry, dashed to the wounded man, picked him up in single movement, and beat a retreat. A rock hit his head and a second spear grazed his shoulder blade. Then he was out of range. That night the Little Men would not yet risk a full struggle.

CHAPTER THREE

A Night in the Swamp

WHEN the son of the Leopard had stirred up the fire, he put the man down on the dry grass and considered him with surprise and wariness. He was extraordinarily different from the Oulhamrs, the Kzams, and the Little Men. From his long thin head grew shaggy hair that was not at all profuse; his eyes were longer than they were wide, and their dark, dull, sad surface seemed to look at nothing. His cheeks were hollow and his jaws weak, the lower one receding like that of a rat; but what especially surprised the chief was

the cylindrical body, almost without shoulders, so that
the arms seemed to grow out like the feet of a croco-
dile. The skin appeared dry and rough as if covered
with scales. The man had not moved since Naoh put
him down on the dry grass. Every now and then his
eyelids lifted slowly and a dull eye focused on the Oulhamrs. His breathing was noisy and hoarse, almost a
whine. He inspired a strong repugnance in Nam and
Gaw. Naoh, being more curious than his companions,
wondered where this man came from, how he happened to be in the swamp, who had wounded him. He
tried to tell him with signs that he would not be killed.
Then he pointed out the screen made by the Little
Men, signaling to him that it was from them death
would come. The man turned his face and let out a
feeble, guttural cry. Naoh felt he had understood. The
crescent moon was high in the sky, from which the
blue had disappeared. Sitting up, the man applied herbs
to his wound; sometimes a feeble glow showed in his
eye.

As the moon darkened, the rays of the stars stretched
across the water and the Little Men could be heard at
work. The Oulhamrs scrutinized the greenish water
with fear and distress while hunger gnawed at their
stomachs.

In the morning glow, the wounded man seemed
stranger still. His eyes were like jade, his long body
twisted about as easily as a worm, his soft, dry hand
bent back bizarrely. Suddenly he grabbed a spear and
hurled it at a water lily; the water splashed, and swiftly

withdrawing the weapon the man brought up a colossal carp. Nam and Gaw let out cries of joy: the fish would suffice for several men's meals. They did not regret that Naoh had saved the life of this strange creature. Energy filled them anew: seeing that once more their leader's action had been beneficent, Nam and Gaw exulted. They no longer feared for their lives: Naoh would figure out how to lay a trap for the Little Men, make them perish in great numbers, and scare off the rest.

The son of the Leopard did not share their hope. He saw no way of escaping. The more he thought about it, the clearer it was that his strategies were useless. He wore them out thinking them over in his mind. He ended by counting on nothing but the strength of his arm and on luck.

CHAPTER FOUR

Combat in the Willows

During the morning the Little Men showed themselves frequently. They clacked their thick jaws in hatred and their triangular eyes gleamed. They brandished their javelins and spears from a distance and made as if to impale the enemies, kill them, crush their heads, and rip open their stomachs.

When the sun was high in the sky the thin man suddenly let out a shrill cry. He got up and waved his arms. A similar cry broke the silence across the swamp. Then at a great distance on the shore the Oulhamrs saw a man exactly like the one they had rescued. He brandished an unknown weapon. The Little Men had also seen him: they immediately sent out a detachment in pursuit, but the man had already disappeared behind the rushes. Naoh continued to scrutinize the area, shaken and confused. For some time they saw the Little Men running across the plains. Soon another group were dispatched. Despite his wounded thigh, the thin man was on his feet; his opaque eyes glowing, he let out a hoarse cry. Events developed fast. Four times more, Little Men were seen circling the swamp and then disappearing. Finally, within some willows and mangroves, around thirty men and women came into view, with long heads, torsoes round and singularly narrow, while the Little Men were revealed on three sides. Combat had begun. When sighted, the Thin Men hurled short javelins, not directly, but with the aid of an object that the Oulhamrs had never seen. It was a thick piece of wood or horn ending in a hook; and this weapon gave the javelins a much greater range than when they were thrown by hand.

At first the Little Men had the upper hand, although a number were stretched on the ground. Reinforcements arrived constantly. Their faces surged from every direction, even from the redoubt opposite Naoh and his companions. A frantic fury drove them on. They dashed straight into the fray with long yells. All the caution that they had shown against the Oulhamrs had gone, perhaps because the Thin Men were familiar to them and they did not fear hand-to-hand combat, perhaps because an ancient hatred drove them on.

Naoh let the enemy entrenchment continue to empty itself. He had made up his mind since the beginning of the combat, without having to ponder a solution. His decision came along with the certainty that the Little Men's triumph would bring his own downfall. He hesitated about one thing alone: should he abandon the Fire? The cage would hamper him in combat; it would undoubtedly be broken in pieces. Also after the victory, fires would not be lacking, and death would follow upon defeat. When he believed the moment favorable, Naoh briskly gave orders, and with a war cry the Oulhamrs sprang out of their refuge at full speed. Several javelins grazed them; already the three warriors had got through the enemy's screen. The contact was rapid and fierce. There were six fighters there, pressed one against the other, hurling spears. Naoh threw a javelin, then bounded in, twirling his club. The Little Men were overcome at the instant that Nam and Gaw entered the fight.

In the willows hand-to-hand fighting had begun. By themselves a few warriors armed with their strange weapons had managed to find shelter in a pond, from which they harassed the Little Men. But the latter had the advantage of numbers and obstinacy. Their victory appeared certain: it could not be snatched from them without a lightning intervention.

Naoh took a long look at the melee. He saw the leader whose voice guided the Little Men, a squat man with hair streaked white, whose teeth were enormous.

Fifteen warriors surrounded him. With the roar of an aurochs, Naoh attacked. Everything in his way fell beneath his club. But near the old warrior, spears bristled; they closed the road, striking at the assailant. He succeeded in beating them down. Other warriors rushed to their leader's defense. Then, calling his companions, with a supreme effort Naoh overthrew the barrier of bodies and weapons and crushed the thick head of the leader like a nut. At the same instant, Nam and Gaw rushed to his aid.

Panic ensued. The Little Men realized that a ghastly energy had overtaken them, and though they would have fought to the last under their leader's direction, they felt abandoned when his voice was silenced. Pellmell, they fled without looking back.

Thirty men and ten women lay on the ground. The majority were not dead. Blood flowed copiously; limbs were broken and heads bashed; bodies bore gaping wounds. A number of casualties would be finished before nightfall. Others would live a few days, and many could be cured. But the enemy must undergo the law of men. Naoh recognized its necessity, and allowed his companions and the Thin Men to pierce their hearts and crush or sever their heads. The massacre was swift; Nam and Gaw hastened and the others acted according to millennial methods almost without ferocity. Then there was a torpid and silent pause. The Thin Men bandaged their wounded. They did this in a more minutely careful and assured manner than the Oulhamrs.

(144)

Naoh had the impression that they knew more than his tribe but that their life was feeble. Their gestures were flexible and slow; they tended a wounded man in twos and even threes; sometimes they were caught in a strange torpor and remained motionless with eyes fixed and arms hanging like dead branches.

The women seemed less slow. They also appeared more skillful and resourceful. After some time, Naoh perceived that one of them even commanded their band. However, they had the same dull eyes, the same sad faces as their men, and their hair was sparse, growing in tufts with spots of scaly flesh between. Several of these women came with two men to tend the wounds of the Oulhamrs. A soft tranquility emanated from their movements. They wiped away the blood with aromatic leaves and covered the wounds with crushed grass secured by straps made from bulrushes. This bandaging was the definitive sign of their alliance. To Naoh the Thin Men seemed much less crude than the Kzams and the Little Men, or even than his brothers.

After being bandaged, the son of the Leopard returned to the granite ridge to recover the fire cage. He found it intact, the little flames still flickering. Seeing them, victory seemed more complete and sweeter still. Not that he feared lack of fire: the Thin Men would surely give him some. But an obscure superstition guided him; he cleaved to these little flames, the fruit of conquest; the future would have appeared menacing if they had died out. Exultant, he brought them back to the encampment.

They observed him curiously, and the woman leader shook her head. Naoh showed by signs that his tribe had seen fire die and that he had managed to reconquer it. Nobody seemed to understand, and he wondered whether this was not one of those miserable races who did not know enough to warm themselves on cold days, put night at a distance, and cook their food. Old Goun used to say that such peoples existed, inferior to the wolves, who surpass men in sharpness of hearing and power of smell. Naoh was going to show them how to make fire grow, when he noticed a woman among the willows striking two stones together. At first sparks flew; then a little red dot danced along a blade of grass that was very tiny and dry; other blades flamed, which the woman kept up softly with her breath: the fire spread to leaves and twigs. The son of the Leopard stood motionless in awe.

He approached the woman to examine the stones. Instinctively she withdrew. Then, recalling that this man had saved them, she held out the stones to him. He felt them; they were cold. Then he took them in his hands and examined them. When he was able to discover no fissure in them, his surprise grew. Anxiously he wondered, "How does the fire get into the stones, and why are they not hot?"

With fear and distrust he returned them to the woman.

CHAPTER FIVE

Across the Land of Waters

THE Oulhamrs and the Thin Men, who called themselves the Wahs, were crossing the land of waters.
Water stretched out in stagnant sheets, full of algae,
water lilies, flowering rushes, loosestrife, rushes, and
reeds. There were troublesome and frightening peat
bogs, lakes, rivers in networks interspersed with layers
of rock, sand, or clay. Water burst from the ground or
flowed down the slopes of hills, and sometimes, drain-
ing into fissures, was lost underground. The Wahs
knew by now that Naoh wanted to take a route be-

tween the north and west. They shortened the journey, wishing to guide him to the end of the humid region. Their resources seemed innumerable. They would discover passages which no other kind of men would have suspected; they constructed rafts, threw tree trunks across ravines, or linked two shores by means of creepers. They were slow but accomplished swimmers, provided that certain plants were not present, of which they had a superstitious fear. Their actions seemed full of uncertainty; often they behaved like creatures struggling against sleep or just coming out of a dream; and yet they almost never mistook the way.

There was an abundance of food. The Wahs were familiar with numerous edible roots, but they especially excelled in catching fish. They could spear them, catch them with their hands, enmesh them in supple grass, attract them at night with torches, and draw schools of them into coves. At night around the fire, they tasted a sweet and silent happiness. The Wahs loved to sit in a group squeezed one against the other, as if their weakness was fortified by the feeling of belonging, while the Oulhamrs preferred to spread out, especially Naoh, who enjoyed long intervals of solitude. Often the Wahs would recite ancient deeds in a monotonous chant which they repeated endlessly. None of this interested the son of the Leopard. But he followed with intense curiosity their actions in hunting, fishing, and direction-finding, and watched with particular attention when they used the projector weapon or drew fire out of stones.

He quickly learned to handle the projector. As he inspired his allies with growing sympathy, they hid none of their secrets from him. He could handle their weapons and their tools, and learned how to repair them, and when projectors were lost, he watched them make new ones. The female leader even gave him one, which he used with as much skill and much more power than the Thin Men. He was much slower at understanding the mystery of fire, because he continued to fear it. He watched the sparks fly from a distance. The questions he put to himself remained obscure and full of contradictions. At first he thought that the Thin Men had imprisoned the fire in the stones. But then he was reassured when he saw sparks drawn out of pebbles that had been lying on the ground. When he was certain that the secret had to do with the things themselves and not with any power of men, his last fears were dispelled. He also learned that to draw sparks two different kinds of stones were needed. And when he had himself made the first spark leap, he tried to light a fire. After gathering a few dry leaves, Naoh struck his stones one against the other. He worked with a violent passion. The blows were so heavy that one of the stones burst in a thousand sparks. A glow stuck on one of the leaves. Then, blowing carefully, he made the flame grow; it devoured its feeble prey and seized other leaves. Motionless, Naoh experienced the greatest joy. He realized that he had just won something more potent than any of his ancestors had possessed and that now the fire would be forever his.

CHAPTER SIX

The Blue-Skinned Men

THE valleys sloped downward still. They crossed land in which the autumn was almost as warm as summer. Then deep forest appeared. A wall of creepers, thorns, and bushes closed it off, through which the Wahs dug a passage. The woman leader let Naoh know that they were not going to accompany the Oulhamrs any farther after they came out into the open again, for beyond that they were unfamiliar with the territory. All they knew was that there was a plain, then a mountain cut in two by a large ravine.

Soon after they entered the forest, the female leader pointed to the undergrowth with a mysterious air. Among the leaves of a fig tree, a bluish body had just appeared in which Naoh recognized the shape of a man. Remembering the Little Men, he trembled with hatred and anxiety. The body disappeared. There was a long silence. Forewarned, the Wahs stopped walking and drew closer to one another. Then the oldest man in the band spoke.

He said that the strength and fury of the blue-skinned men was terrible and that above all they must avoid taking the same route as they were passing through their camp. He added that they detested noise and gestures.

"Our fathers' fathers," he concluded, "lived in their neighborhood without war. They yielded the way to them in the forest. And the blue-skinned men in their turn avoided our fathers' fathers in the plain and on the waters."

Changing direction, the band moved through a forest of sycamores and finally came out in a large clearing. Suddenly Naoh discerned to the right a figure like the one he had seen among the leaves of the fig tree. Two other forms in succession could be made out in the sea-green shadows. Branches rustled and a supple and powerful creature emerged. No one could tell whether it had come up on four feet like the hairy beasts and reptiles or on two feet like birds or men. It seemed to squat with its hind legs half stretched out on the ground and its front limbs set back, poised on a thick root. Its face

was enormous, with the jaws of a hyena, round eyes
that were alert and full of fire, a long, low cranium, and
a deep torso like a lion's, only larger: each of its four
limbs ended in a hand. Dark hair, shining tawny and
blue, covered its whole body. It was from the chest and
shoulders that Naoh recognized a man, for the four
hands made it a singular creature and the head recalled
a buffalo, bear, or dog. After turning a wary and angry
face in all directions, the blue-skinned man rose up on
his legs and let out a cavernous growl.

At this, similar creatures sprang pell-mell from cover.
There were three males, a dozen females, several little
ones who were half hidden in the roots and grass. One
of the males was colossal, with gnarled arms like a plane
tree and a chest twice as vast as Naoh's; he could over-
throw an aurochs and strangle a tiger. He carried no
weapons, but among his companions two or three held
leafy branches with which they scratched the earth.

The giant advanced toward the Wahs and the Oulhamrs while the others grunted in a group. He struck
his chest and the white mass of his teeth could be seen
gleaming between the heavy, trembling lips. At a sign
from the female leader, the Thin Men beat a retreat.
This they did without haste; obeying an ancient tradition, they abstained from any gesture or word. Naoh
imitated them, having confidence in their experience.
But Nam and Gaw, who were in front of the band,
remained indecisive for an instant. When they tried to
imitate their leader, the way was barred. The blue-
skinned men had spread out in the clearing. Gaw

(153)

dashed into the undergrowth while Nam tried to cross
a clear space. He slipped so lightly and furtively that he
almost succeeded. But with a bound a female rose up
before him; he swerved. Two males ran up. While
skirting them, he stumbled. Two enormous arms seized
him: he found himself in the hands of the giant. He had
not had time to lift his weapons; an unbearable pressure
paralyzed his shoulders and he felt as weak as a saiga
under the weight of a tiger. Then, aware of the distance
which separated him from Naoh, he remained stunned,
his muscles immobile and the pupils of his eyes red.
The young man grew weak from the certainty of
death.

Naoh could not stand to see his companion killed; he
advanced, but the chief stopped him. She made him
understand that if he were to strike, Nam would perish.
He was caught between his intent to fight and his fear
of seeing the son of the Poplar crushed. He let out a
hoarse sigh and watched. The blue-skinned man had
lifted Nam: he ground his teeth, swung him, ready to
crush him against a tree trunk. Suddenly he stopped
moving. He looked at the inert body, then at the face.
Sensing no resistance, his terrible jaws relaxed and a
vague softness came into his wild eyes; he placed Nam
on the ground. Had the young man made a move to
defend himself or shown terror, the terrible hand
would have seized him again. He knew this instinctively and remained immobile. The entire band, males, females, and little ones, and gathered around. They all
recognized confusedly in Nam a structure analagous

to their own. For the Little Men or the Oulhamrs this would have been a strong motive to kill, but those blue-skinned creatures were strangers to war, they did not eat flesh, and they lived without traditions. Before Nam, they remained full of uncertainty. His immobility appeased them, and they became less and less inclined to bite or strike him. As he had felt the breath of destruction, now Nam sensed that his peril had lessened. He sat up slowly and waited. For a moment they continued to observe him with a distant defiance; then a female, tempted by a tender shoot, thought of nothing but eating it; a male began to dig up roots; little by little they all obeyed the deep need for nourishment. As they drew all their strength from plants and as their choice of food was more restricted than that of the elks or aurochs, the task was long and continual.

The young Oulhamr was free. He rejoined Naoh, who had advanced in the clearing, and still shaken from the adventure, both watched the blue-skinned men disappear into the forest.

CHAPTER SEVEN

The Giant Bear Is in the Gorge

AFTER a long march, Naoh and his companions crossed a notch in the mountains where they parted from the Thin Men. Soon after, they were out on the plateaus. There the autumn was cooler, endless clouds rolled across the sky, winds blew incessantly, and grass and leaves decayed on the miserable earth.

Naoh, Nam, and Gaw hardly ever suffered from hunger. The journey and its adventures had sharpened their instinct, skill, and wisdom. They could spot prey at a distance just as they could tell the enemy's presence. They could foresee wind, rain, and flood. Each of their actions was adroitly adapted to an end and they used energy economically. With one look they could trace a favorable line of retreat, a safe resting place, or good terrain for combat. They could orient themselves with almost as much assurance as migratory birds. Despite mountains, lakes, stagnant waters, forests, and floods which changed the lay of the land, they got closer each day to the land of the Oulhamrs. Now they hoped to rejoin the band within a few days.

Among many roads Naoh had chosen a long gorge which he remembered having passed through with a hunting party when he was Gaw's age. Part of the gorge was hollowed between chalk cliffs and part opened into a ravine, ending in a sharply sloping corridor where rock-slides often had to be climbed. The warriors passed through it without mishap until they were two-thirds of the way. Toward the middle of the day, they sat down to eat. It was in a semicircular area, a crossroads of crevasses and caves. They heard the roar of a subterranean torrent falling into an abyss; two dark holes opened into the rock which showed the traces of cataclysms more ancient than any living species.

When Naoh had finished eating, he headed toward one of these caverns and looked at it a long time. He remembered that Faouhm had shown his warriors an opening through which there was a quicker way to the plain. But the slope, full of loose rocks, was not fit for climbing by a numerous group. It ought to be possible for three light men; Naoh wanted to try it. He went to

the back of the cave, recognized the fissure, and went into it far enough to see a dim light that indicated a nearby exit.

On his return he met Nam, who said to him, "The giant bear is in the gorge!" A guttural call interrupted him. Dashing to the entrance of the cave, Naoh saw Gaw, concealed among some rocks in the attitude of a warrior stalking prey. And the leader shivered with fear. At the entrances to the circular area two monstrous beasts appeared. They had extraordinarily thick coats the color of oak, which protected them against the coming winter, thorns, and the harshness of the rocks. One of them was as massive as an aurochs, with short paws that were muscular and flexible and a swollen forehead like a rock covered with lichen. His vast jaws could snap the head off a man and crush it. The female had a flat forehead, shorter jaws, and a sideways gait. "Yes," murmured Naoh. "These are giant bears."

They feared no creature. But they were to be feared only when they were enraged or driven by excessive hunger, for they did not live off meat very much. They growled, and the male raised his jaws and shook his head violently. "He is wounded," Nam remarked.

Blood flowed over his coat. The Oulhamrs were afraid that the wound was made by a human weapon. In that case the bear would look for revenge. Once he began an attack, he would not abandon it: no creature was more stubborn. With his thick coat and tough skin, he defied javelins, axes, and clubs. He could rip a man open with a single blow of his paw, strangle him with

(159)

one grip, chew him to pieces with his jaws.

"Where did they come from?" asked Naoh. "From between those trees," replied Gaw, pointing to some fir trees growing on hard rock. The male came from the right and the female from the left. By chance or vaguely thought-out tactics they had managed to bar the exits of the gorge. Attack seemed imminent. It was evident from the rough voice of the male and the sly, concentrated attitude of the female. They were still hesitating because they thought slowly and their instinct required certainty; they sniffed the air with long, deep breaths to measure better the distance of the enemies hidden among the rocks. Naoh gave his orders abruptly. When the bears got started, the Oulhamrs were already at the back of the cave. The son of the Leopard made the young men go first; all three hurried as fast as the rough ground and the detours of the passage permitted.

Finding the cave empty, the giant bears lost time identifying the trail among the tracks the Oulhamrs had already left. At times they stopped, full of mistrust. For if they feared no living being, they had a great natural caution and a confused fear of the unknown. They were familiar with the uncertainty of the rocks, caves, and abysses; their tenacious memories held the image of falling and crumbling boulders, ground giving way, deep gulfs, avalanches, and water hollowing out levels of stone. In their already long lives, no mammoth, lion, or tiger had threatened them. But strange forces sometimes thwarted them: they carried the sharp

(160)

marks of stones; they had almost disappeared beneath snows, and had felt themselves carried off by the torrents of spring and held captive beneath landslides. Now that very morning, for the first time, creatures had attacked them. It was at the top of a sheer rock which only lizards and insects could climb. Three vertical animals were standing on the top. At the sight of the giant bears, they had let out a cry and hurled sharp sticks. One of them wounded the male, who, disoriented by pain and rage, lost his clear-sighted instinct and tried to get directly to the summit. He quickly gave this up, and followed by his female, tried to find roundabout access. On his way he tore out the javelin and sniffed it. Memories came to him. He had not often encountered men, but the sight of them did not surprise him any more than wolves or hyenas. As they had got out of his way, he was familiar with neither their tricks nor their traps and was not worried by them. This unforeseen adventure was more troubling. It disrupted the order of things and introduced an unexpected menace. The bear roamed on through the passages, trying slopes and attentively sniffing the sparse scents. At length he grew tired. Without his wound he would have kept only the vague memory that sleeps beneath the flesh and does not awaken until similar circumstances irritate it. But twinges of pain from time to time brought back images of the three men standing on the summit, and of the sharp weapon. Then he would growl and lick himself. Soon the pain ceased to recall the image. The giant bear thought of the difficult search for food as he sniffed the men's odor. Rage filled his chest. He signaled to his female, who had taken another way, for they could not both sustain themselves, especially in cold weather, on surfaces that were too close. And after assuring himself of the position and distance of the enemy, he launched the attack.

In the dark fissure, Naoh at first was only aware of the presence of his companions, then the heavy tread of the brutes could be heard and their powerful breathing: the bears were gaining on them. They had the advantage of being balanced on four limbs gripping the ground, with their nostrils grazing the trail. Constantly, one or the other of the Oulhamrs would bump into a stone, stumble in a pothole, hit a projection of the wall; and they had to carry weapons, provisions, and the fire cages, which Naoh refused to abandon. As the little flames burned very small at the bottom of the cages, they did not light up the road; their feeble reddish light lost itself in barely pointing out the formations on the cave ceiling. At the same time it threw weird distortions of the fugitives' shadows.

"Quick! Quick!" cried the leader.

Nam and Gaw could not take a straight course, and the giant beasts were approaching. At each step their breathing could be heard more clearly. Their fury grew as they felt the enemy closer, now one, now the other letting out a growl. Their great voices echoed among the stones. Naoh got a better idea of their enormous structure, their terrible grip, and the irresistible tearing of their jaws. Soon the bears were only a few steps away. The earth vibrated under Naoh, whom an immense weight would soon crush. He faced his death. Suddenly pointing the cage, he aimed its dim light at a vibrating mass. The bear stopped short. The surprise woke his caution. He considered the little flame vibrating over his paws, and let out a hollow call to his female. Then fury overcame him and he dashed upon the man. Naoh drew back, and hurled the cage with all his strength. It hit the bear's nose and burned one eyelid. He let out a roar of pain, and as he was collecting himself, Naoh gained ground.

A gray light filtered into the caverns. Now the Oulhamrs could make out the ground beyond: they were not stumbling any more, but running at high speed. The beasts resumed pursuit, redoubling their speed, and as the light grew stronger the son of the Leopard sensed that in the outside air the danger would become stronger.

Once more the giant bear was close. His burning eyelid had revived his rage, and all cautiousness had left him. His head swollen with blood, nothing could stop him. Naoh could feel his presence from the deep breathing and brief, harsh growls behind him. He was about to turn and fight when Nam let out a cry for help. The leader saw a high projection which made the passage smaller. Nam had already passed it and Gaw was sidestepping it. The bear was growling three paces behind when Naoh in his turn slipped through the gap, hunching his shoulders. His speed carrying him forward, the beast knocked himself against the wall and only his immense muzzle passed through the opening. He gaped, showing his teeth that were like scythes and grindstones, and letting out a great, sinister clamor. But Naoh was no longer afraid, being suddenly at a distance the beast could not cross: the stone, stronger than a hundred mammoths and more durable than the life of a thousand generations, arrested the bear as surely as death itself. The Oulhamr gloated.

"Naoh is now stronger than the great bear. For he has a club, an axe, and javelins. He can strike the bear; the bear cannot return the blow."

He had raised his club. At this, the bear recognized the mountain traps he had fought against since his childhood. He withdrew his head before the man struck, and hid himself behind the rock projection. His anger remained, expanding his ribs and beating against his temples, pushing him to impetuous action, but he did not yield to it. For he was led by a sagacious instinct which did not ignore circumstances. Since that morning, he had on two occasions realized that man could inflict pain with strange blows. He began to accept his fate, a painful work was begun which would later result in his placing these vertical beings among the things that were dangerous. The female bear, less experienced than her wounded male, growled at his side. When the male's cry indicated that caution was necessary, she stopped advancing, imagining some trap on the other side of the rock. For she could not imagine that any peril could come from these puny creatures hidden around the wall.

CHAPTER EIGHT

The Rock

THE descent was rough. Autumn had multiplied the slides and fissures. The three men made use of axes and javelins. When they reached the plain the last obstacle was crossed; all that remained was to follow easy trails well known to them.

They walked till evening: Naoh was looking for a bend in the river where he wanted to make camp. The day was dying under heavy clouds. A red glow floated over everything, sinister and morose, accompanied by the howling of wolves. These moved about in furtive bands, stalking along the edge of bushes and trees. Their number astonished the Oulhamrs. Some exodus of herbivorous animals must have driven them from neighboring territories and brought them together in this land rich in prey. They seemed to have exhausted it. Their clamor indicated penury, and their speed a feverish activity. Knowing that they were to be feared in great numbers, Naoh hastened his course. At length two packs were formed, on the right and on the left. As the shadows blotted out the sunset, their eyes showed more clearly; Nam, Gaw, and Naoh perceived a multitude of little green fires darting about like fireflies. The warriors often retorted to the howls with long war cries, sending ripples through this mass of phosphorescent dots.

At first the wolves kept out of range of the javelins, but as the shadows grew darker, they came closer; the soft noise of their paws could be heard more distinctly. Some of them had gotten ahead of the men. They would stop abruptly, leap with sharp cries, or crawl in a sly manner. The others came up behind, their voices tearing the air. They had grown furiously impatient. In the last light of the evening, the two packs oscillated like waves of palpitating flesh and breakers of noise. At length, the stubborn pursuit worried the men. Facing the almost darkened west among so many sly beasts, they sensed the presence of death.

A group of wolves went ahead of Gaw, who was walking on the left, and one of them stopped, showed his gleaming teeth, and leaped. The young man ner-

(166)

vously hurled his spear. It pierced the beast's side, and it somersaulted with a long howl; Gaw finished it off with a blow of his club. At the death cry the wolves flocked around. Naoh feared the attack of the whole pack. He called Nam and Gaw to him to intimidate the beasts.

The Oulhamrs made their stand close together; surprised, the wolves furled about them like waves. If one had dared to rush them, all the others would have followed and the bones of the men would be bleaching on the plain. Brusquely Naoh hurled a javelin; a wolf fell to the ground, his chest gaping. Seizing him by his hind feet, the leader threw him among a group which were bearing down on them on the right. The wounded animal disappeared among them, and the odor of blood attracting the famished beasts, they started devouring his living flesh. In the ensuing melee, the three men raced off. A haze indicated that the river was near by — at intervals Naoh saw it sparkling. Two or three times he stopped to get his bearings. At last, pointing to a grayish mass rising above the bank, he said, "Naoh, Nam, and Gaw can laugh at the wolves."

It was a great rock almost in the shape of a cube, rising to five times the height of a man. It was accessible from only one side. Naoh climbed it rapidly, having been familiar with it for many seasons. Following him, Nam and Gaw found themselves on a flat surface sprinkled with bushes and an occasional fir tree. Thirty men could camp there easily. Over toward the ash-gray plain, the wolves fought wildly. Ferocious rumbles, long cries, and snarls were heard in the humid air. The Oulhamrs enjoyed their security.

The wood crackled as the fire darted its red tongues, sending up smoke and spreading a wide glow over the water. From the solitary rock two segments of bare riverbank extended. Rushes, willows, and poplars grew at a distance, so that everything could be made out for a range of twenty javelin throws.

Beasts were fleeing and hiding from the brightness or running up to it in fascination. Two screech owls flew into an aspen with eerie cries, a cloud of bats billowed, a wild flight of swallows wheeled on the other shore, frightened ducks left cover and flew into the darkness, long fishes surged up from the bottom like silver smoke, arrows of mother-of-pearl, and coppery spirals. The red glow also revealed a stocky boar, who stopped and grunted, a large elk, his spine quivering and his head and antlers thrown back, the sly head of a lynx with triangular eyes, coppery and ferocious, appearing between two branches of an ash tree.

The men were aware of their security. In silence they ate roasted meat, living happily in the warmth of the fire. The band was near! Before two nights they would see the waters of the Great Swamp. Nam and Gaw would be welcomed as warriors: the Oulhamrs would know of their courage, guile, and long patience, and they would fear them. Naoh would have Gammla for his reward and would command after Faouhm. They thrilled with hope, and if their thought was short, their instinct was prodigious, full of deep and precise images.

Suddenly Nam started. With his back turned to the fire, his gaze followed a reflection on the other shore which played on the water, slipping among the willows and sycamores. And with his hand outstretched, he murmured, "Son of the Leopard, some men have come!"

A heavy feeling came over Naoh, and all three of them concentrated on the spot. But the banks were deserted, and nothing was heard but the lapping of water. All that could be made out were animals, grass, and trees.

"Was Nam mistaken?" asked Naoh. The young man, sure of what he had seen, replied, "Nam was not wrong: he saw men's bodies among the willows — there were two." The leader doubted no more. He said softly, "This is the country of the Oulhamrs. Those you saw are hunters or scouts sent out by Faouhm."

He stood up and stretched. It would be no use to hide: friends and enemies would be too aware of the significance of the fire. He cried out, "I am Naoh, son of the Leopard, who has conquered Fire for the Oulhamrs. Let Faouhm's scouts show themselves."

The solitude remained impenetrable. Even the breeze had died down and the roars of wild animals. Only the crackling of the fire and the fresh voice of the river seemed to expand.

"Let Faouhm's scouts show themselves!" the leader repeated. "If they look, they will recognize Naoh,

Nam, and Gaw! They know they will be welcome."

All three standing before the red fire showed silhouettes as visible as in plain day, and let out the call of the Oulhamrs.

Waiting. It gnawed the hearts of the three companions. It implied all the terrors of life. And Naoh muttered, "They are enemies!"

Nam and Gaw knew it well and all their joy left them. The peril that struck them that night was harder, since their return seemed so close. It was more equivocal since it came from men. On this ground near the Great Swamp they had only expected their people's approach. Had Faouhm's conquerors attacked them again? Had the Oulhamrs disappeared from the earth? Naoh saw Gammla conquered or dead. He ground his teeth and threatened the other shore with his club. Then he squatted by the fire in despair, thinking and waiting. The sky had darkened in the east and the moon in its last quarter had appeared across the savanna. It was red and flaming. It was still weak but its light reached the shadows of the site: flight, which Naoh was meditating, would be almost impossible if the hidden men were numerous and if they had laid an ambush. As he thought, a great shiver shook his body. Downstream, he had just noticed a stocky figure in silhouette. Although it disappeared rapidly into the rushes, certainty pierced him like the point of a spear. The men who were hiding were Oulhamrs to be sure, but Naoh would have preferred Kzams or Little Men. For he had just recognized Aghoo the Hairy.

CHAPTER NINE

Aghoo the Hairy

In the space of several heartbeats, Naoh relived the scene when Aghoo and his brothers had stood before Faouhm and promised to conquer Fire. Menace flamed in their eyes, strength and ferocity were in their gestures. The Oulhamrs had listened to them with trepidation. Each of the three brothers would have stood his ground to Faouhm. With their chests as hairy as a gray bear, their enormous hands, their arms hard as oak branches, with their guile, skill, courage, their indestructible solidarity, they were each worth ten warriors. Thinking of all the men they had killed, a boundless hatred contracted Naoh's heart. How was he to beat them? He, the son of the Leopard, believed himself the equal of Aghoo: after so many victories his self-confidence was complete; but Nam and Gaw would be like leopards faced with these lions! Surprise and conflicting emotions had not delayed Naoh's resolution. It was as rapid as the bound of a deer surprised in its shelter.

"Nam will leave first," he commanded, "then Gaw. They will carry spears and javelins. I will throw them their clubs when they are at the base of the rock. I will carry only the fire." For in spite of the mysterious stones of the Wahs, he could not resign himself to abandon the conquered flame.

Nam and Gaw understood that they must get ahead of Aghoo and his brothers before they could rejoin the tribe. Hastily they seized their arms, and Nam was already on his way down the escarpment, Gaw following at the level of twice a man's stature above him. When Nam was almost at the bottom, a cry of terror burst from the bank, succeeded by a bellowing, then the screech of a bittern. Leaning over the edge of the platform, Naoh saw Aghoo leap out of the rushes. He came at full speed and an instant later his brothers dashed out, one from the south and the other from the east. Nam had just leaped onto the plain. At this point Naoh felt his heart full of trouble. He did not know whether he should throw Nam's club to him or call him back. The young man was more agile than the sons of the Aurochs, but while they were converging on the rock he would pass within range of a javelin. After a brief hesitation the leader cried, "I will not throw the club to Nam — it will weigh down his escape! He must flee! Let him warn the Oulhamrs that we are waiting here with the fire."

Trembling, Nam obeyed, for he knew himself to be weak before these formidable brothers who had gained ground on him during his short pause. After several bounds, he stumbled and had to regain his balance. Seeing his danger growing, Naoh recalled his companion. Already the hairy ones were near. The most agile hurled his javelin. It pierced the young man's arm at the moment he began to climb the slope; the assailant let out a war cry and rushed on Nam to crack his skull. Naoh was waiting. With his awesome arm he threw a stone: it made an arc in the half-light and cracked the enemy's femur, bringing him to the ground. Before the son of the Leopard had chosen a second projectile, the wounded man disappeared behind a bush, letting out roars of rage.

Then there was a great silence. Aghoo went over to his brother and examined his wound. Gaw helped Nam to get back on the platform; Naoh, on his feet in the double light of the fire and the moon, raised a piece of porphyry in his two hands and stood ready to pelt the aggressors. He spoke first: "Are not the sons of the Aurochs of the same tribe as Naoh, Nam, and Gaw? Why do they attack us like enemies?" Aghoo the Hairy stood up in turn. He let out a war cry and replied,

"Aghoo will treat you like friends if you will give him his share of the Fire, and like elk if you refuse him." A snarling laugh came from his jaws; his chest was large enough for a panther to sleep on. The son of the Leopard cried, "Naoh has conquered Fire from the Kzams. He will share the Fire when he has rejoined the tribe."

"We want Fire now. Aghoo will have Gammla, and Naoh will receive a double portion of prey and booty."

Fury shook the son of the Leopard. "Why should Aghoo have Gammla? He was not able to conquer Fire! All men have mocked him."

"Aghoo is stronger than Naoh. He will rip you open with his spear and break your bones with his club."

"Naoh has killed the gray bear and the tigress. He has killed ten Kzams and twenty Little Men. It is Naoh who will kill Aghoo!"

"Let Naoh come down into the plain!"

"If Aghoo came alone, Naoh would have gone to fight him alone."

Aghoo's laughter exploded like a roar: "None of you will see the Great Swamp again!"

Both were silent. Shivering, Naoh compared the slim torsos of Nam and Gaw to the fearful structures of the sons of the Aurochs. Yet didn't he have an advantage? For if Nam was wounded, one of the three brothers was incapable of pursuing an enemy. Blood flowed from Nam's arm. The leader applied ashes to it and covered it with herbs. As he watched, he asked himself how he would fight. It was impossible to surprise Aghoo's and his brothers' vigilance. Their senses were sharp and their bodies tireless. They had strength, guile, skill, and agility. A little slower than Nam or Gaw, they surpassed them in range. Only the son of the Leopard was swifter and had more endurance. The situation was piecing itself together in Naoh's head, and gaining coherence by his instinct. Thus he could see the ins and outs of the flight and combat; he was already all action while he remained squatting in the copper glow. At last he got up and a sly smile flickered in his eyes; he stamped out the fire like a bull pawing the ground. First the fire must be put out so that, even if they were the victors, the sons of the Aurochs would not have Gammla or the ransom. Naoh threw the thickest brands into the river; with the help of his companions he killed the fire with earth and stones. He only kept alive one of the feeble flames in the cages. Following this, he organized the descent. This time, Gaw would go first. At the level of two men's height he would stop on a ledge large enough to keep his balance, and throw javelins. The young Oulhamr quickly obeyed. When he got to the assigned spot, he called softly to warn his leader.

The sons of the Aurochs had joined battle. Aghoo faced the rock, his spear in his hand; the wounded man, standing against the bush, held his weapons ready; and the third brother, Rouk the Red-Armed, who was closer than the others, moved back and forward in a circle. Standing on a ledge jutting from the platform, Naoh sometimes leaned over toward the plain and sometimes brandished a javelin. He seized the moment when Rouk was closest to hurl his weapon. It covered the distance, which astonished the son of the Aurochs, but it needed a length five times a man's height to hit its mark. A stone which Naoh threw next fell at a lesser distance. Rouk let out a sarcastic call: "The son of the Leopard is blind and stupid." Disdainfully, he raised his club in his right hand. Furtively Naoh grabbed a weapon prepared in advance: it was one of those projectors he had learned to use among the Wahs. He gave the sling a quick turn. Rouk, sure that this was a menacing gesture, continued his walk with a hoot of laughter. As he was no longer facing the rock, the light was not certain and he did not see the javelin coming. When he saw it, it was too late; his hand was pierced at the thumb joint. With a cry of rage, he let go of his club.

Aghoo and his brothers were stupefied. The range Naoh had attained far surpassed their expectation. Feeling their power diminished before a mysterious trick, all three withdrew. Rouk had not been able to pick up his club in his left hand again.

Meanwhile, Naoh profited by their surprise to help Nam get down; the six men found themselves on the plain, alert and full of hatred. Suddenly the son of the Leopard cut to the right, where the passage was larger and more reliable. There Aghoo barred the way. His circular eyes watched each of Naoh's gestures. He was marvelously coordinated to dodge the javelins. He advanced in the hope that his adversaries would use up

(176)

their projectiles in vain against him, while Rouk came
up swiftly after him. But Naoh pulled up short,
swerved abruptly, and threatened the third brother who
was leaning on a spear, waiting. This movement forced
Rouk and Aghoo to head to the west; now there was
more space. Nam, Gaw, and Naoh rushed ahead without having to fear that they would be within range.

"The son of Aurochs will not have fire!" the leader's
voice resounded. "And Naoh will take Gammla."

All three were fleeing across the plain; perhaps they
might have reached the band without combat, but
Naoh realized it was necessary to risk death for death
that very night. Two of the hairy ones were wounded.
To run away from the fight was to give them time to
heal, and the peril would return more dangerous than
ever. In this first phase of the pursuit, even Nam, in
spite of his wound, had the advantage. The three companions gained another thousand feet. Naoh stopped,
handed the fire to Gaw, and said, "You must run without stopping toward the sunset until I rejoin you."

They obeyed, continuing at the same speed, while
the leader followed more slowly. Soon he turned around,
faced the hairy ones, and threatened them with the
projector weapon. When he judged them close enough,
he cut toward the north, past their right flank, and
headed straight for the river. Aghoo understood. He
let out a roar like a lion and backtracked with Rouk to
the aid of the wounded warrior. Desperately he gained
a speed equal to Naoh's. But this speed exceeded his

(177)

build. The son of the Leopard, better built for high speed, regained the advantage. He arrived near the rock with an advance of three hundred feet, and found himself face to face with the third brother.

He looked formidable as he waited. He hurled a javelin. Off balance, he missed his aim, and already Naoh rushed on him. The strength and skill of the hairy one were such that in spite of his paralyzed leg he could have beaten Nam or Gaw. To combat the great Naoh he made a more powerful assault: the blow of his club was so strong that it would have taken his two legs to sustain the kick, and while he stumbled his adversary's weapon came down on the back of his neck and knocked him to the ground. A second blow broke his spine.

Aghoo was now a hundred feet away; Rouk, weakened by the flow of blood from his hand and less agile, was a hundred feet behind. Both arrived at their goal like rhinoceroses, carried forward by so deep an instinct of race that they forgot all strategy.

With one foot on the vanquished, the son of the Leopard awaited them, his club ready. Three feet away, Aghoo bounded in attack. Naoh had slipped away. He ran after Rouk with the speed of an elk. With a final motion, swinging his club with both hands, he struck Rouk's weapon which he had raised maladroitly in his left hand; then, with a blow on the head, he knocked down the second antagonist. Running off once more from Aghoo, he cried, "Where are your brothers, son of the Aurochs? Have I not killed them as I killed the gray bear, the tigress, and the Kzams? And here I am as free as the wind! My feet are fleeter than yours, my wind stronger than an elk's!"

Having regained his advance, he stopped and watched Aghoo coming. He said, "Naoh does not want to flee any more. This very night he will take your life or give his own."

He took aim at the son of the Aurochs. But his enemy had recovered his guile: he slowed up and remained watchful. The javelin whistled through the air. Aghoo ducked and the weapon whizzed over his head.

"It is Naoh who is going to die!" he yelled.

He hurried no more; he knew that this adversary was free to accept or refuse the fight. His furtive gait inspired fear. Each of his movements resembled a beast of combat; death was carried with him in the shape of the spear and the club. Despite the victory over his brothers, he did not fear this great agile warrior with swift arms and broad shoulders, for he was stronger than his brothers and had never known defeat. No man or beast had been able to resist his club. When he came within range, he hurled the spear. He did it because he had to; but he was not surprised to see Naoh dodge the sharp point. And Aghoo dodged the enemy's spear in turn.

Now there was nothing but the clubs. These were raised simultaneously; both were made of oak. Aghoo's had three knots; it had been polished with time and

gleamed in the moonlight. Naoh's was more rounded, less old, and dark in color. Aghoo struck the first blow. He did not put all his strength into it; it was not in this way that he hoped to surprise the son of the Leopard. So Naoh got out of the way without difficulty and took a sideswipe. The other warrior's club met the blow; the wood bashed together with a tremendous crack. Then Aghoo leaped to the right and came back on the great warrior's flank: he dealt the immense blow which had broken the heads of men and beasts. It encountered emptiness, while Naoh's club came down on his. The shock was so great that Faouhm himself would have reeled; Aghoo's feet held their ground like roots. He was able to leap backward.

Thus they found themselves face to face with no wounds, as if they had not been fighting. But all the strength they possessed they put into the struggle. Each recognized in the other a formidable adversary; each knew that if he weakened for the space of a moment's motion he would enter death.

Aghoo resumed combat with a hoarse yell. All his strength passed into his arm: he brought down his club without feint, resolved to crush all resistance. Withdrawing, Naoh opposed his weapon. He deflected the blow but could not keep a knot from making a large gash in his shoulder. The blood spurted, turning the warrior's arm red. Aghoo, sure of destroying once again a life which he had condemned, raised his club; it came down in a fearsome blow.

The rival had not waited for the club to come down,

and the momentum threw the son of the Aurochs forward. Letting out a sinister cry, Naoh returned the blow. Aghoo's head rang like a block of oak, his hairy body staggered; another blow brought him to the ground.

"You shall not have Gammla!" roared the conqueror. "You will not see the band or the swamp, and never again will you warm your body by the fire!"

Aghoo got to his feet. His hard head was red, his right arm hung like a broken branch, his legs no longer had any strength. But stubborn instinct glimmered in his eyes and he took up the club with his left hand. He brandished it for a last time. Before it struck, Naoh knocked it ten feet out of his hand. And Aghoo awaited death. Already it was in him; he did not understand defeat otherwise; he remembered with pride all the creatures he had killed before succumbing himself.

"Aghoo crushed the head and the heart of his enemies," he murmured. "He never left alive anyone who disputed booty or prey with him. All the Oulhamrs trembled before him."

The cry came from his obscure consciousness, and if he had been able to rejoice in his defeat he would have done so. At least he felt virtue in never having shown mercy, always annihilating the danger that is the rancor of the vanquished. So his days seemed to him without reproach. As the first death blow hit his head he let out no cry; he cried only when thought had left him and he was nothing but warm flesh, which Naoh's club stilled in its last quiverings. Then the conqueror went to finish off the two brothers. And it seemed to him that the power of the sons of the Aurochs had entered into him. Turning toward the river, he listened to his heart booming. Time was his! He no longer saw any end to it.

CHAPTER TEN

The Endless Night

E ACH day at sunset the Oulhamrs would wait in anguish for the departure of the sun. When only the stars were left in the heavens or the moon was buried behind clouds, they felt strangely puny and miserable. Huddled in the darkness of a cavern or beneath an overhanging rock, faced with the cold and evening shadows, they dreamed of the Fire which used to nourish them with its warmth and keep off the fearsome beasts. The watchers never ceased to hold their weapons ready; fear and strained attention harassed their brains and bodies: they knew that they could be taken by surprise before being able to strike. A bear had devoured a warrior and two women; wolves and leopards had carried off some children; many of the men bore scars of nocturnal combat.

Winter was coming. The north wind hurled its spears; under clear skies frost bit them with sharp teeth. And one night Faouhm, the chief, in a struggle against a lion, lost the use of his right arm. Thus he became too weak to impose his command, and disorder grew among the band. Houm no longer wished to obey. Mouh claimed to be first among the Oulhamrs. Both had their partisans, while a small number remained faithful to Faouhm. However, an armed struggle did not take place, for all were tired: the old man Goun reminded them of their weakness and of the peril that would result if they killed each other. They understood him: in the hour of shadows they had bitterly regretted the missing warriors. They despaired of seeing Naoh, Gaw, and Nam or the sons of the Aurochs. Several times search parties were sent out: they came back without having discovered any trail. They became fearful of the worst, that the six warriors had fallen beneath the claws of wild beasts or the axes of men, or that they had perished from hunger. The Oulhamrs would never again see the helping Fire alive!

In spite of greater sufferings than the males, the women alone maintained an undefined confidence. That patient resistance which is the salvation of races subsisted in them. Gammla was among the most energetic.

Neither cold nor hunger impaired her youthful vigor. In winter her hair grew longer; she tossed it about her shoulders like the mane of a lion. Faouhm's niece had a profound knowledge of plants. On the prairie or in the reeds she could spot roots, fruit, and edible mushrooms. Without her the great Faouhm would have perished during the days when his wound kept him laid up in a cave, exhausted by the loss of blood. Fire did not seem to her as indispensable as to the others. Still she desired it passionately, and at the beginning of each night she wondered if it would be Aghoo or Naoh who would bring it back. She would be ready to submit, since respect for the stronger was deeply instilled in her; she did not conceive that she could refuse to be the wife of a conqueror, but she knew that life with Aghoo would be harder.

An evening approached that looked frightening to the band. The wind had dispelled the clouds. It passed over the withered grass and black trees with a long howl. A red sun as large as the hillside still lit up the site. And in the twilight which was about to disappear into endless time the band assembled, shivering with fear. It was weak and mournful; when would the days return when flames crackled as they ate up the logs? Then an odor of roasting meat used to rise into the evening, and a warm happiness came into their bodies, as pitiful wolves prowled about, and bears, lions, and leopards moved away from this sparkling, living thing.

The sun sank and in the bare west the light faded. Old Goun, whose misery had grown with the years, let out a disquieting moan. "Goun has seen his sons and the sons of his sons. Never did the Oulhamrs lack Fire. Now there is no more Fire, and Goun will die without seeing it again."

The hollow of the rock in which the band was sheltered was almost a cavern. In good weather it might have been a suitable shelter, but now the wind whipped their bodies. Goun continued: "The wolves will become more daring each night." Furtive shadows multiplied with the fall of night. The howls were longer and more menacing; night poured out its famished beasts. Only the last glimmer of twilight still kept them at a distance. Anxiously the watchers walked in the harsh air beneath the cold stars . . .

Suddenly one of them stopped and cocked an ear. Two others imitated him. Then the first declared, "There are men in the plain!" A shiver passed through the band. With some of them fear dominated; others were filled with hope. Remembering that he was still chief, Faouhm got up from the fissure in which he was resting. "Let all the warriors have their weapons ready!" he commanded.

The Oulhamrs silently obeyed. The chief added, "Let Houm take three young men and see who is coming."

Houm hesitated, displeased at receiving orders from a man who had lost the strength of his arm, but old Goun interposed: "Houm has a leopard's eyes, a wolf's ears, and a dog's power of smell. He will know if the men approaching are enemies or Oulhamrs."

(187)

So Houm and three young men set out. As they advanced the wild beasts fell upon their tracks. They were soon out of sight. For a long time the tribe waited in misery. Finally a long cry cleaved the darkness. Bounding onto the plain, Faouhm yelled, "They are Oulhamrs who are coming!" A terrific emotion pierced all their hearts. Even the little children got up. Goun stated what he and all the others were thinking: "Is it Aghoo and his brothers . . . or Naoh, Nam, and Gaw?"

New cries resounded under the stars.

"It is the son of the Leopard!" Faouhm murmured joyfully. For he feared the ferocity of Aghoo. But the others thought only of the Fire. If Naoh brought it back they were ready to kneel to him; if he did not, hatred and disdain would meet his weakness.

At last Naoh was in sight. He arrived like a black shadow on the gray plain, and Faouhm cried, "The Fire! Naoh brings Fire!"

There was a tremendous commotion. Some people stood stock still as if struck by an axe. Others leaped about with frantic yelps. And the Fire was there.

The son of the Leopard held it in a stone cage. It was a little red glow, a humble light that a child could crush with a stone. But everyone knew the immense strength that was going to spurt from this feeble being. Panting and mute, frightened of seeing it die out, they fed their eyes on its image. Then there rose up a cry so loud that the wolves were frightened. The whole tribe pressed about Naoh with gestures of humility, adoration, and compulsive joy.

"Don't kill the Fire!" cried old Goun as the clamor abated. Everyone spread out. Naoh, Faouhm, Gammla, Nam, Gaw, and old Goun formed a nucleus in the crowd and walked toward the rock. The tribe gathered dry grass, reeds, and branches. When the bonfire was ready the son of the Leopard brought the frail light close to it. It caught at a few twigs at first; spitting, it began to devour branches; then, roaring, it swallowed up logs.

Speaking to the great Faouhm, Naoh asked, "Has not the son of the Leopard fulfilled his promise? And will the chief of the Oulhamrs carry out his own?" He pointed to Gammla, standing in the red glow. She shook her long hair. Flushed with pride, she had no more fear. She participated in the admiration in which Naoh was enveloped by the tribe.

"Gammla will be your wife as was promised," Faouhm replied almost humbly.

"And Naoh will command the tribe!" old Goun declared boldly. He spoke thus not out of disrespect for the great Faouhm, but in order to destroy rivalries he considered dangerous. In this moment when fire had just been reborn, no one would dare contradict him. Exultant approbation welled up on every face. But Naoh saw only Gammla; her long hair and fresh, lively eyes spoke the language of his race. A profound indulgence toward the man who was going to bestow her upon him rose in Naoh's heart. Still, he understood that a warrior with a useless arm could not command the

Oulhamrs alone, and so he cried, "Naoh and Faouhm will lead the tribe."

In their surprise, everyone was quiet and for the first time Faouhm felt his ferocious heart invaded by a confused tenderness for a man who was not his own blood. Meanwhile, old Goun, by far the most curious of the Oulhamrs, wanted to know the adventures of the three warriors. They were throbbing in Naoh's brain, just as alive as when he had so recently lived through them. At that time words were few, their consistency weak, their power to evoke short, brusque, and intense. The great warrior spoke of the gray bear, the giant lion and the tigress, the Kzams, mammoths, Little Men, Thin Men, blue-skinned men, and the great cave bear. However, out of distrust and guile, he omitted the secret of the fiery stones which the Wahs had taught him.

The roaring flames confirmed his narrative; by crude gestures Nam and Gaw emphasized each episode. Because it was the discourse of the conqueror, it struck to the depths of all their beings and made their hearts beat. And Goun cried, "There is not a warrior comparable to Naoh among our fathers — and there will not be one among our children nor our children's children!"

Finally, Naoh pronounced the name of Aghoo; his listeners trembled like trees in a storm. For they all feared the son of the Aurochs. "When did the son of the Leopard see Aghoo again?" Faouhm interrupted with a distrustful look at the shadows.

"One night ago," replied the warrior. "The sons of

the Aurochs crossed the river. They appeared before the rock where Naoh, Nam, and Gaw were camped. Naoh fought them."

Then there was a silence in which not even the tribesmen's breathing could be heard. All that could be heard was the fire, the breeze, and the distant cries of beasts.

"And Naoh defeated them," the warrior proudly declared. The men and women looked at one another. Enthusiasm and doubt conflicted in their hearts. Mouh expressed what they all were obscurely asking, "Did Naoh kill all three?"

The son of the Leopard answered nothing. He plunged his hand into a fold in the bearskin that enveloped him and tossed onto the ground three bloody hands. "Here are the hands of Aghoo and his brothers!"

Goun, Mouh, and Faouhm examined them. They could not be mistaken. Enormous and thick, the fingers covered with hair like a wild beast's, they evoked irresistibly the formidable bodies of the hairy ones. Everyone recalled having trembled before them. Rivalry was extinguished in the hearts of the strong braves; the weak identified their lives with Naoh's; the women sensed that the race would endure. And Goun the dry-bones proclaimed, "The Oulhamrs shall fear no more enemies!" Seizing Gammla, Faouhm prostrated her before the conqueror and said, "There. She shall be your wife. And my protection is no longer upon her. She shall kneel before her master. She shall go in search of

(192)

the prey that you will kill and shall bring it back on her shoulder. If she disobeys you, you may put her to death."

Naoh, placing his hand on Gammla, gently raised her up, and what seemed like time without end stretched out before them.